BEAUTY RISING

JIM ABLE OFFWORLD
BOOK 1

ED CHARLTON

Subscribe to Ed's monthly newsletter!
edcharlton.com
Free eBook for new subscribers.

Books in the ***Jim Able Offworld*** trilogy
Beauty Rising, Larc Ascending, Time

Books in the ***Assassin*** trilogy
Book One, Book Two, Book Three

Books in ***The Aleronde Trilogy***
The Problem with Uncle Teddy's Memoir, Saint John's Ambulatory, Aleronde the Great

and
Hoyle Station

CONTENTS

Able — 1

Chapter One — 3

Chapter Two — 10

Chapter Three — 22

Chapter Four — 37

The File — 55

Sopha — 72

Chapter Five — 73

Chapter Six — 84

Chapter Seven — 96

The File, Part Two — 98

Chapter Eight — 109

TMV — 118

Chapter Nine — 119

Chapter Ten — 133

Chapter Eleven — 156

A'nir — 165

Chapter Twelve — 166

Chapter Thirteen — 175

Chapter Fourteen — 186

Chapter Fifteen — 196

Epilogue and Prologue — 212

First Contact Claim Form — 214

Next Time: Larc Ascending — 217

You Might Also Like — 219

Hoyle Station — 221

Newsletter — 223

JIM ABLE OFFWORLD

ABLE

1

ED CHARLTON

AUTHOR OF "THE ALERONDE TRILOGY"

PRELUDE

Turcanis Major:
Fourteen planets, including two gas giants.
Planet Five is habitable, no sentient life, but has two moons, one of
which is home to a technological race.

The Pocket Atlas of Known Space, p. 656

When the sky is spread with reflection,
and water-rushing rises below,
night-flames flicker pale in supplication,
then all are called by Beauty to believe.

Margrev Aplar of the Second Order

CHAPTER ONE

Jim Able's small spacecraft held position above the northern pole of Turcanis Major V. A tethered transceiver array floated listlessly from the ship's rear. As the planet spun slowly below, the craft adjusted its orientation—keeping in view TMV-I, the largest moon.

Five Earth days, three and a half TMV days, or seven TMV-I days had passed, depending on how he counted it. Whichever one, he should have been moving in. He should have chosen his contact by now.

Jim still thought that his boss, Liz Curacao, was wrong. There was no evidence that the trader known as "Edward" was sponsored by the Turcanian government; he appeared to be a lone entrepreneur.

Watching Turcanian television, Jim worried that he'd not seen any mention of a space program on news shows so far. He could be walking into a first contact situation, not a second. He knew he had to be careful—given the sensitivities that new races always have about aliens. And, after the lecture Liz had given him at the briefing, he had another reason to be careful; jobs like his were hard to come by.

. . .

Jim was watching, over and over, a recording he'd made of a recent comedy show.

Three members of a Turcanian family are talking in their living room. A fourth enters the room, possibly the youngest of the family. He is wearing a hooded blue cloak, similar to "Edward's." The audience buzzes as he walks on stage. The father says, "Oh no, take that off! You're not going to the marshes!"
The audience roars with laughter, and the boy reluctantly takes off the cloak.

"Why is this funny?" Jim asked aloud. He shook his head.

Lucy Fry's people had put together a good training class in the Turcanian language and culture. Good enough, in fact, to give Jim a clear understanding of news programming. Comedy, alas, was another matter.

He added to his notes.

Is blue robe indigenous to the marshes?

Is "going to marshes" equiv. leaving home? Like knotted handkerchief & stick?

He intended to show this scene to his contact and ask the question directly. It bothered him. It fascinated him.

He sighed and stopped the playback. He still needed to find his contact. No, he still needed to *choose* his contact. He had the names of many leading politicians; one religious leader; and someone he thought was a judge, but the translation of the office was ambiguous.

The politicians were problematic. TMV-I society enjoyed many political parties and endless rounds of debates and voting. Choosing a party's leader could be seen as an offworld endorsement of that party. He needed someone independent, preferably someone with scientific credibility.

He glanced up at a grainy head-and-shoulders picture of Edward taped up in the cockpit. He looked at the bare, bumpy head, the forehead extending over the eyes. "For someone so ugly, you've sure caused a lot of trouble."

From his lonely vantage point, Jim Able went back to watching live television.

The cockpit seat was uncomfortable for a long trip like this, and his mind drifted. The first flier at the rental agency had been great. It had had a state-of-the-art cockpit. It had had a sleeping berth. It had had paint. It had gleamed in the faint sunlight. It had stunk.

They had tried to disguise the smell, probably spraying deodorizer until the controls were dripping. But it only took one inexperienced pilot to throw up in an unexpected moment of zero-G, and nothing cheap would fix the odor.

So, he had taken the other one: scarred, burnt, cramped—but functional. It had a combined decontamination/shower/toilet unit, often referred to as the shit-shave-shower-shpecial. His seating choice was there or the cockpit; there was nowhere else to go.

He lowered the back of his seat to lie flat. The sound of alien speech rolled over him as he drifted off to sleep.

He woke to a voice, high-pitched and whiney, delivering its words in an overly rapid fashion. Jim scratched his head and sat up. The TV show, a panel discussion, featured a solemn-voiced moderator, two shifty-looking politicians, and the owner of the voice, clearly a female.

As he listened, Jim began to smile. The Turcanian was a scientist. She mentioned her own show, so she was a TV personality of some sort. She was also making the politicians squirm.

"You idiots are so engrossed in your petty arguments you never look up! You've forgotten the whole of the rest of the galaxy that's out there. When are you going to quit wasting our money and leave some resources for science? Especially astronomy! You're making self-aggrandizing decisions at the expense of our whole species. It's pathetic!"

"Hello," Jim said to the face on the screen. "I represent the rest of the galaxy."

He watched until the show ended and the moderator was thanking his guests.

"...Professor Madhar Nect, of the Latsin Institute, presenter of *Science World*, [something that didn't translate] of Gullara."

"Okay, Ms. Madhar Nect," Jim said, "you have my attention. Expect the unexpected."

He set about making breakfast. The plan for initiating contact would take some time to work through. He wanted to be wide-awake and undistracted.

The first part of the plan was to acquire some Turcanian currency.

Gornna Finance was offering a credit account with no background checks. That sounded good. To qualify, all Jim needed was an address. He flipped through his notes. In a kids' TV show, he had learned how to form addresses.

He targeted the flier's transceivers on one of TMV-I's communication satellites. He set the hacking program to mimic a call from a land-based voice communicator.

After several tries, he heard a steady tone over his headset. He entered the number for the Gornna Finance special offer. He heard several tones and, then, a Turcanian voice.

"You are using a voice-only unit. Please call again with a voice-text unit."

"Oh, okay," said Jim, quietly. "How do I do that?"

It took an entire day—and two more children's programs—to discover the kind of machine he needed. The VTU was a hybrid telephone and keyboard. Jim cannibalized one of the flier's internal diagnostic units that had a keypad, but he had little confidence that the communication protocols were similar. After several hours of poring over data streams, he had finally tricked the diagnostic unit into talking somewhat like the Turcanian system. He again entered the number for his special offer.

The information required was brief: name, address, age, and political party.

He entered *james able, arturn 53 latsin trofa, 33, meblish nrc.*

Then he filled out a form he didn't understand. He made up some answers and hoped for the best.

———

THANK YOU FOR DOING BUSINESS WITH GORNNA FINANCE.
YOUR CREDIT ACCOUNT NUMBER IS 15-344-1296-43569.
YOUR ACCOUNT EXPIRES ON MAK 24 ORLAT.
YOUR CREDIT IS MP20.000,0.
YOUR IDENTIFIER IS 565692. DO NOT DISCLOSE YOUR IDENTIFIER TO
ANY UNAUTHORIZED PERSONS.
A REPRESENTATIVE WILL CALL TO COMPLETE THE LEGALLY REQUIRED
DOCUMENTATION. PLEASE ASK THE REPRESENTATIVE ANY QUESTIONS
YOU HAVE ABOUT YOUR ACCOUNT OR OTHER GORNNA FINANCE
SERVICES.

———

"Thank you," said Jim, smiling in relief. "How very trusting of you."

Part two of the plan involved spending, or at least promising to spend, some Turcanian currency.

TMV-I was awash with electronic communication. The TV commercials revealed a fierce marketplace for an increasingly over-served customer base. FooStur was Jim's chosen target. The name was a pun on the words for "fast" and "commune." He only needed a few days of electronic text transmission. FooStur specialized in helping travelers temporarily away from their regular communication providers. *Just like me*, Jim thought.

He called FooStur's number. The temporary VTU came to life again. This time both voice and text were used. It was Jim's first conversation with a real Turcanian. She said he had a Multoaf accent and asked if he knew her sister in Trell.

All he had to do was type in his credit account number. She did the rest. He was now *jim Vable Vfoostur Vax Vgam.*

He had one difficult moment when she thought his name was strange and asked him to repeat it a couple of times. She said something he didn't catch, and he let it pass. He made a mental note to replay the conversation and listen more closely to what she had said.

Part three of the plan was simply to send Madhar Nect an electronic message.

———

madharVnectVlatsinVux

Greetings, Madhar Nect.

I enjoyed your recent TV appearance.

I wish to meet you.

I am not from your planet.

Please indicate a private place where we can meet without publicity.

jimVableVfoosturVaxVgam

———

The reply was simple.

———

jimVableVfoosturVaxVgam

Don't waste my time. The fake ID doesn't impress. Who are you really?

madharVnectVlatsinVux

———

madharVnectVlatsinVux

I understand your suspicion.

When it is midnight tonight at the Latsin Institute, watch the position five miles above the northern pole of the planet you orbit. I will signal three times in quick succession.

jimVableVfoosturVaxVgam

———

Jim programmed the thrusters to flare, front and back, three times —bright enough for Nect to see, but not strong enough to knock his small flier out of position. Jim's fears that Nect would not be watching were relieved within two minutes.

———

jimVableVfoosturVaxVgam

Neat trick.

I'm interested to know how you did it. Rockets? Mirrors? For that, I'll meet you.

Tomorrow I'm going to my retreat. It's in Martorn, the last house on the peninsula. Take the dirt road on the right after the mall. Arrive in the evening.

madharVnectVlatsinVux

———

madharVnectVlatsinVux

I won't be driving. I've found Martorn and its peninsula on a map. I'll need a flat area about 25 by 25 partel. Please advise.

Expect me after sunset. Thank you.

jimVableVfoosturVaxVgam

———

jimVableVfoosturVaxVgam

Okay, persist in your nonsense.

The western field by the dock is larger. Don't hit the power lines, spaceman.

madharVnectVlatsinVux

———

Jim thought he would make up part four of the plan when he got to Martorn.

CHAPTER TWO

He watched night roll over the edge of the continent where the community of Martorn was located and waited until the last possible moment to move toward the moon from his vantage point above the planet.

Avoiding two satellites, he descended into the atmosphere of TMV-I. For part of the journey, a weather system shielded him from view. For the last part, it was clear sky all the way. He was painfully conscious of leaving a visible entry path through the atmosphere.

Madhar Nect sat on her dock, listening to the warblers calling each other over the quiet, black water of the bay. She listened for the vehicle that she knew was coming. She had even guessed which student was playing games with fake messages. Something flickered in the sky, out to sea beyond the bay, but it didn't last long enough for her to be sure she had seen it.

For many minutes nothing changed. The warblers fell silent. The gentle lapping of small waves seemed to grow louder. A faint hissing sound grew in the air. She looked up to see that a vapor trail had formed over the water. Its leading edge boiled the damp air. It was coming lower toward her.

Her face rigid in astonishment, Madhar Nect saw the hissing

cloud dissolve, leaving a black shape hovering over her field. Bright lights turned everything monochrome for a few seconds. Then, with a cough of power, a craft settled onto the ground amid a shimmer of smoke and vapor.

Jim stepped out of the flier's decontamination unit, opened the hatch, and lowered the ramp. The air was thick with moisture and strongly scented by Turcanian flowers. He let his eyes adjust to the dark.

He saw Madhar Nect standing out on the dock. He moved forward slowly toward her. "Good evening, Madhar Nect. I am Jim Able. Thank you for allowing this meeting."

The scientist gave a formal reply. "Good evening, Jim Able. Welcome to my home. You traveled well?"

"My travel was good. I thank you."

They paused after the formula was exhausted. The two aliens stood scrutinizing each other.

Jim was struck by how much smaller the scientist looked in person. On the talk show she had seemed tall and thin. In fact, her head barely reached the level of his shoulder.

"Would you like to see my craft?" Jim volunteered.

The scientist only nodded. They walked around to the front of the still-steaming flier. Jim gave a few of the operational details.

"You...go...," began Madhar, "you go into space in *this*?"

Jim looked at his craft. It really did not look in good shape. The burned metal was a history of neglect.

"This perhaps isn't typical of modern spacecraft."

"Ah."

There was another pause.

"Can you," Madhar asked, staring again at Jim, "eat our food?"

"I've been looking forward to it."

"Come inside, Jim Able. Welcome."

They walked side by side into the scientist's home. It was a small two-story building. It looked as if it had been built from timbers cut on the property. The doors were simple painted boards, and what looked like plaster walls were decorated with photographs. Some pictured groups of students; several, Jim noticed, were taken outside on the dock. There were also family groups, recognizable from the formality of the poses.

"Why have you come, Jim Able?"

"To see you."

Madhar smiled, unconvinced.

Jim continued, "I need to make contact with someone in your government. This is really an official visit. But your politics are confusing to an outsider. So, I thought you could help guide me. I don't want to cause any alarm or be involved in any publicity. It's a small matter that should not take long."

"Our politics are confusing to us too. It must be a 'small matter' of great importance for you to travel—I would guess enormous distances—to be here, in fact, to be the first alien ever to visit us." The scientist reflected, "If, as we suspect, there are many inhabited worlds, many races, surely making contact with a new one is something to be handled very carefully?"

"Indeed. And that's really at the heart of the 'small matter.'"

Jim paused. He was not sure about divulging all he knew, yet. "One of your race has already made contact with us."

Madhar was silent for a long while. "How?"

"He has traveled, in a better-looking craft than mine, to a number of inhabited worlds."

"A government representative?"

Jim smiled. "That is what I would like to find out. We're interested in developing relations and opening avenues for trade, and we pay substantial rewards to individuals who play key roles in making that happen."

Madhar shook her bumpy head and made a buzzing noise. "It's not possible that the government could have built a spacecraft and kept it secret—perhaps some of the military could. But, even then, I would know at least someone whom they would have contacted for expertise. One person, did you say?"

"Just one."

"Why one? I would have a minimum of four on any expedition." She looked at Jim. "That anyone would risk space travel alone is astonishing."

Jim smiled. "Sometimes no one will go with you."

The scientist cocked her head and narrowed her eyes. "Like visiting a small race of no particular note?"

"I'm glad I didn't visit a politician first."

They both laughed—in their different ways.

"I will help you if I can, Jim Able, but I don't hold out much hope. It can't be a government-sanctioned activity. We have to look to business, I think. But…" She gave Jim another strange look. She stood up and brought out a rectangular device. "Will you allow me to record part of our conversation?"

"Of course. As far as we are concerned, the niceties of isolation and initial contacts are, if not behind us, at least fuzzy. Your traveler has no doubt told tales of his experiences. Rumors can be dangerous. If I can help to bring out the truth, I will. Please record me. Ask me anything you like. We want to welcome you to the galactic community. Though I would rather not have this particular visit delayed by immediate publicity."

Madhar set up her device and began to question her guest.

"How do you come to speak our language? Do you know you sound like you're from Multoaf?"

"We've monitored your transmissions for a while. Your educational programs were very useful. I've been watching a lot of your TV."

"Oh no! What must you think of us?"

"Out there, we try to communicate using a created language called Standard. I'll leave a training unit here with you that you are welcome to replicate and distribute."

"How has our 'traveler' been able to communicate?"

"He claims to have learned Standard from listening to local space traffic."

"How has he done that? I've been listening for offworld signals for years and never heard a thing!"

"Well, the frequency bands we use normally are here and here on the spectrum." Jim drew a rough sketch on a piece of paper. "No, the only place long-distance signals are possible is down here. Up here, the interstellar noise wipes out anything else."

"It begins there, yes, but above here it clears again and there's a huge sweep of clean frequencies."

"Aargh!" the scientist threw her head back and said something Jim did not understand.

"I must remember to ask you later. My vocabulary is limited in its range of polite, or impolite, expletives."

Madhar nodded. "I work with students; they are a constant source of new profanities. Have no fear," she jabbed her finger at him and smiled. "We'll have you sounding like you're from Trofa yet."

As they talked, she served him a warm citrus-flavored drink and some small tasteless bread-like lumps.

"How do you manage to travel astronomical distances without growing old?" she asked.

"Hmm," Jim nodded. "The whole galactic trading network is only possible because of one thing—the D-switch."

"The what?"

"D-switch. It's a small device that lets you enter in three relative spatial coordinates. You engage the device, and it takes you there."

Madhar was not buying it yet. "Go on."

"The time at which you engage the switch is the same time that you arrive at the new coordinates."

The scientist swore again. "You have time machines?"

"No! I don't know much about them, really! I just use them. But space-time is four dimensions. The theory is these things are doing something in the fifth or some higher dimension. It's the galaxy's dirty little secret. Not only do people like me not know how they work, but being within the confines of space-time, we *can't* know how they work. They're performing some extra-dimensional activity, and maybe it's just a side effect. Anyway, it is damned useful to us."

Madhar was staring at Jim, much as she had when he first stood in her field.

Jim went on, "The way it was explained to me was this—you're familiar with there being other dimensions, right?"

"Of course! Mathematically speaking."

"Right. Imagine we were just three-dimensional beings. I know the analogy doesn't really hold up, but try explaining sculpture to someone who doesn't experience time. All they'd know is you're talking about an object being itself, and then—whatever 'then' means—a strike with a chisel and it is two objects, large bit over here, small bit over here."

"Ouch," she muttered, frowning.

"These switches are doing something we can't imagine. The effect we see is movement in space with no accompanying movement in time. In fact, if there is time taken during the traveling, and the time is reversed when we arrive, how could we know? It may be —must be—an activity like sculpture that we, from our vantage point, can't hope to understand. We just see the result."

"So which smart-ass invented, or discovered, it?"

Jim shook his head. "Like I said, it's the galaxy's dirty secret. We didn't. There is one supplier. They are an...odd...life-form. We normally don't have dealings across that kind of barrier. In fact, we all tend to keep to our own groups: primates like you and us are more comfortable with other primates, reptilians with reptilians, and so forth. These guys are really different. And even they were given the first switches. We don't know anything more than that. It was a long time ago. They only sell them to legitimate ship makers, who embed them in appropriate navigation systems. As I said, I use them; I don't really get into it apart from that."

"Well, it makes me more comfortable, in a way, that you guys out there don't know it all. But it also makes me very scared of how much we've got to learn."

She thought for a long while in silence. "Are there limits to how far you can go?"

"Sort of. They have a really short range relative to interstellar distances. But think about it: you can just keep D-switching over and over. It doesn't take any time. The only time taken during a journey is for the navigation unit to recalculate and set the next coordinates. It does add up; it took me a couple of weeks to get here."

"Do you use them for personal transport on your world?"

"No, you can only use them in empty space. You need to get away from the gravity wells of star systems. From what I hear, the flatter the space, the longer the range. That's why we still carry other kinds of propulsion—chemical thrusters, solid fuel burners, ion drives, whatever—for local travel."

"What happens if you try it? I'm sure it's the first thing I'd try if I had one!"

"It doesn't take you anywhere. Or, if it does, it isn't enough to notice."

"And these 'odd' folks aren't talking, huh?"

"You don't risk upsetting them, or the ship makers for that matter. It's a monopoly, and business is business. No one wants scientific curiosity to get in the way of that."

"So, some things are the same out there as they are down here." She smiled sadly but did not elaborate.

Madhar went into the small kitchen to prepare some more food. Jim stood and looked more closely at the pictures on the walls. He noticed that the pictures of students on the dock, aside from the obvious informality, had one thing in common: Madhar was almost doubled over with laughter in every shot. He had seen her laugh a little, exposing her neat rows of triangular teeth, but the scenes on the dock were of unbridled mirth that evoked in Jim both admiration for her and a quiet sadness for himself.

He looked out of the corner of his eye as she worked at the kitchen table. Her hands, with the typical Turcanian look of supple leather, were making rapid, accurate movements, chopping something that looked like cheese. He thought of the contrast between the scientist at work and at play: between the precision and the abandonment. Still a novice at reading Turcanian facial expressions, he guessed the wrinkling of her brow indicated that her mind was fully occupied with forming a question for him while her hands were busy about other things. Jim saw that her forehead was less pronounced than Edward's. Her eyes, human-like in their brightness and keen intelligence, were less hidden. They gave her round face an open quality that spoke of approachability. Jim guessed that her students loved her.

As she worked in the kitchen, Madhar tried to calm herself. She had to keep a clear head to absorb the wealth of technical information coming from the alien. She knew well how to project a calm exterior. She had delivered lectures and demonstrations before large crowds of students, occasionally with unpredicted results. She had hosted live episodes of *Science World* during which she had grappled with everything that threatened to push affairs into chaos. She had done these things within the confines of the people and world she knew. This was different. She was discovering more than any one scientist ever had a right to find in one lifetime. But she felt she was missing things. There were too many questions to ask and too few points of reference from which to launch them.

She hated to admit to herself that part of the problem was how ugly the alien appeared. She was annoyed at herself for even letting such considerations enter her mind, but the reaction was there to be dealt with. She felt that the similarities of physique were a reasonable basis for overcoming her negative feelings. Had they had a similar evolution? Jim had referred to their both being primates. Madhar wasn't sure if that would hold up to close scrutiny. Perhaps the possibility alone was sufficient for her to see the commonality.

She glanced at Jim as he studied the pictures on her wall. It was the hair. *How could any self-respecting creature go around with that disgusting knot of hair pointing in such confused directions?*

Turcanians had lost the fur of their ancestors several subspecies ago. To appear on this moon with hair was to declare oneself a throwback to the aggressive and the primitive. Yet Jim Able was neither. She was glad he had decided to come first in secret. There were many who would have reacted badly to such a creature if it had suddenly appeared in the center of a city.

Madhar remembered the appopo she had sat watching in the zoo months before. Appopo were the nearest branch on the evolutionary tree. There was nothing in its behavior to say it had any intelligence; any creature can scratch itself or pick up a stick and chew on it. But to do it while keeping eye contact with a stranger beyond the glass and have the encounter be one of mutual study took true intelligence. It was in the appopo's eyes that she had understood its intentions. It was in the first flash of Jim's eyes in the dark of the field that she had understood the same. His head might look like a balloon with a small rug on it, but inside was a creature her equal, if not more.

She steeled herself to put such things aside and to return to gathering every piece of knowledge she could, regardless of her visitor's appearance. This was a night to grasp hold of with both hands. She felt more excited than if she had been elected to rule the world.

"How do you communicate over the distances?" she asked.

"That's another really useful application of the D-switches—the communications relays. There's a network of communications devices serving trading partners. They kind of sit out there, switching back and forth constantly, making a way of communicating instantly."

"But don't they drift? I mean, everything in the galaxy is in constant motion."

Jim shrugged. "Yeah, I guess so. Like I say, I'm a user, not an engineer."

"Hmm," she said, gazing far off. "What happens if someone hits one or uses this D-switch to go to the same space that something else occupies?" She sat back, holding up both hands in a gesture he had seen her use on the talk show. She waited as if she were going to catch his answer.

"You're responsible for checking that there's nothing already there. That's an advantage of the limited range; you don't need to have most of your ship given over to long-range sensors. But it could be fatal, I suppose. Some substances can take a sudden increase in density without too much trouble—there's a lot of interatomic distance. Live tissue has more difficulty with foreign objects suddenly appearing in the middle of it. But no two D-switches will hit the same space at the same time. That's what I hear. I haven't wanted to try it."

"No, I can imagine. What bothers me—apart from suddenly being in a very different galaxy from the one I woke up in this morning—is what have we got that anyone else would want? We're a small fish in this enormous pool. And if we do have something worth anything to other races, what's to stop them—or you—just coming in and taking it?"

"That's really how I come to be here."

"Go on.

"I work for the Office of External Affairs, which is part of Sol Earth's—that's the name of my home planet—Earth's Department of Extra-Solar Activities. I'm a bureaucrat."

"How dull! I thought you were an explorer or a diplomat."

"No," he laughed, "I got involved because there is a dispute about who gets the reward for making first contact with you. I have two competing claims on my desk. There's a premium to be gained by getting to a new race before anyone else. You can make exclusive deals and cut out the competition from the other races. My world is still fairly new in the game. We pay big money for the chance to get in first. I get to deliver the money, when appropriate, to the person who makes such an introduction. Now, of course, there's also a risk in each first contact. If it's not handled right, you can open hostilities rather than trade. If a smaller race feels threatened, they can easily overreact. That's when everyone else takes notice."

"Yes, you said about the rewards."

"You know what happens when you have a battle between spaceships?"

"What do you mean?"

"Imagine I'm in a ship like that one out there, and I fire a rocket with an explosive warhead at you in your ship."

"Okay..."

"Suppose I destroy you. What happens to your ship?"

"It breaks up. I die."

"It breaks up into billions of tiny pieces, all endowed with explosive velocities. They are a menace to everyone until they embed themselves in something else. You just hope that something isn't you or your equipment. Now just suppose, as happens a lot in the heat of a battle, my rocket misses your ship. What then?"

"It'll keep going in the direction you fired it until it gets caught in the gravitational influence of a planet or star."

"That's right. Space is big. It can keep going for a long time until it hits something."

The scientist looked into the distance, frowning. "We have some problems with space debris in orbit. Our satellites occasionally get punctured by bits that dropped off earlier ones or, as you say, from explosions. We've had a few missions that went wrong. But rogue munitions are a terrifying prospect."

"So, the other side of paying out First Contact fees and opening up trade with a new race is talking to them, watching what they do and what they purchase, and making sure they aren't going to do anything stupid that will adversely affect everyone else."

"Ah!" she said, smiling. "You're a spy as well as a bureaucrat!"

Jim smiled back. "The official term for me is 'officer of information.'"

"Got it. Maybe you're not so dull after all."

She made Jim feel comfortable with his choice of contact. The scientist and her visitor amicably talked most of the night away.

As dawn approached, Jim said, "I would rather take off again before anyone notices where I parked. As I said, I don't want to be delayed by a media event."

Madhar shook her head. "No one will see your ship here. This is all my property around us. I discourage uninvited visitors. My life is all too much in the public gaze. I retreat here when I can and keep my privacy."

"For all our talk, I still don't know who to contact next about my lone trader."

"Come with me, and we'll concentrate on just the one problem."

Madhar led Jim out to the dock. She reached down for a line and drew up from the water a cage filled with writhing, shiny black bodies. She unhooked the line and brought the box and its squirming contents up to a low table set under the extended eaves of the house. She lit a small fire and put a long rectangular pan over the flames.

"Blancar," she told Jim, "are the real reason I come here. You have to eat them now or they spoil."

She tipped them all into the pan and splashed a purple liquid over them. The sizzling and popping were too loud to talk over for several minutes.

"Let's go over what you know about him again."

"Sure. He called himself 'Edward.' We refer to your star as Turcanis Major. Once he knew that, he called himself 'Edward of Turcanis.' He wanted, and eventually bought, a high-definition infrared scanner and associated equipment."

"Okay, what does 'Edward' mean?"

"It's a name. I suppose it does mean something; I don't know that I remember. Maybe 'guardian' or something like it. 'Prosperous guardian,' I think."

Madhar shook her head. "Doesn't help. Okay, what good is a high-definition infrared scanner?"

"It'll pinpoint small heat sources, potentially over long distances."

Madhar shook her head again. "Perhaps we could survey our world from a satellite and learn something from such a device, but it's not something we've needed yet. I can't see why he'd want one."

After a few more minutes of gently frying, the blancar were ready. Jim's apprehension gave way to delight. They were a sweet and tangy fish with no discernible bones. After several helpings, he began to wonder if they were not more worm than fish.

"I have an image of Edward."

Madhar gave him a sly smile. "There are nearly two billion of us. I don't think I'll recognize him."

Jim showed her the picture. The effect was startling. Madhar laughed, and half a mouthful of blancar sprayed over the table.

"He's a Regdenir! Why didn't you say so? He's a Barottin Regdenir!" With one hand she was hitting the table as she swept the bits of blancar off with the other.

Still laughing, she said, "You've come a long way for nothing, I'm afraid."

CHAPTER THREE

"What is a Regdenir?" Jim asked.

"You don't want to bother with them. That lot! They're tree-climbers!" Madhar replied.

"Tree-climbers?"

"Yes. Dreamers. Crazy people. You don't need to bother."

Jim had so many questions he became momentarily inarticulate.

"Look," said Madhar, "they are...an embarrassment. They all dress like that, with the hooded blue cloak. They've done it for centuries. They're throwbacks to our past. They live in their own little world, clinging to ancient beliefs. They worship Mainworld. Literally. It's a god to them. It's very embarrassing that he's become our first representative to the galactic community."

"You call the planet Mainworld?"

"Sure, what else would you call it? I suppose the only other name would be Magg, but that's archaic now."

"Okay. Slowly now, he's part of a religious community?"

"Yeah, it goes back a long way. They don't allow intermixing. They despise the general population. They have been aggressive about it in the past. They all live out in the tidal marshes on the west coast."

"The marshes?" Jim said, sitting up suddenly.

"What about them?"

"I saw something on a comedy show. A kid put on a blue cloak, and his father said something about 'not going to the marshes.' It was funny, apparently."

Madhar smiled. "Well, yes, it is. They're symbolic for us. If we didn't have the Regdenir, we'd have to invent something like them. They are the 'them' that makes us 'us,' you understand? It doesn't help that they are incredibly rich."

"How so?"

"From the marshes. When the Regdenir migrated out there three or four centuries ago, it wasn't good. Many of them died. You see, Mainworld gives us enormously powerful tides. There are vast underground lakes under the west coast. At high tide, much of that water percolates up through caverns and cracks and floods the marshes. The valleys out there are never dry, even at low tide. If it were just the seawater, it wouldn't be so bad, but all that extra subsurface water makes it an extreme place to live. Well, anyway, they survived and began to build conduits for the water, learning to harness the latent power of it all. They set up vast electricity genera-tors. They got their own back on us; our technological revolution was founded on that power. And they make us pay for it. Literally."

"So it's not that they don't take part in modern life?"

"No, they pick and choose, in ways that make no sense. They won't use television, but they have one of the biggest computer networks that has ever existed. What do they do with it? I don't really know, but I know they've loaded all their Holy Scriptures into a vast database. As I said, they're crazy."

"So, Edward is a Regdenir."

"A Barottin Regdenir. There were other varieties of Regdenir, but these are the only ones who didn't intermix."

"Okay. Let's redraw the question. What does a Barottin Regdenir need a high-res IR scanner for?"

Madhar smiled again. "You don't realize how funny that ques-tion is."

Jim was, again, at a loss.

"They are a law unto themselves, my alien friend. Asking why they do anything is like asking a blancar why it pops in the pan! Give it up. Go home. Absolutely give up on talking to anyone in government about him. They'd laugh you back into space."

Jim looked out across the lake. "How can I find him?"

Madhar shook her head slowly. "How did you find me?"

"Do they have their own messaging system?"

"No. We have theirs. But, of course, they do things slightly differently. The address format is the same: first name, 'V' for a separator, second name, separator, then where we have institution or business or government department, they have level of authority within their religion. The teachers and prophets are 'Regde1,' poets and thinkers are 'Regde2,' and so forth; I don't know the full story. You watch television. Find a documentary about them; they are always making them. The fourth part of the address is the community, I think. They have several quite large towns."

"But you've no idea how I can find *him*?" Jim pointed at the image again.

"No. Not a clue."

They sat in silence for a while as the sunlight sparkled through the trees and caught the soot rising from the dying fire.

"Is there anyone in the government who has regular contact with them? Someone in charge of the buying of electricity, perhaps?"

Madhar shook her head again. "It's not so simple. Alliances come and go, and they are experts at playing us off against each other. Wait a moment."

She went inside the house. Jim waited and savored the morning on this strange little world. He liked it.

His host returned with an address on a small piece of paper.

wehorulan Vjiir Vregde4 Vapp

"This is the only one I have had contact with recently, and that was two years ago. He wanted my help in boosting transfer rates in an older generation of computer chips. I couldn't help much. He might know how you can trace your 'Edward.'"

"Thank you. I'll send him a message."

"That's something I was going to ask. How did you get into our message system?"

"I opened an account."

"But how did you pay for it?"

"A nice credit agency gave me a number."

"But you need an address for that!"

"There's a really short period when you can use your account to put down a deposit before they come and find you. They'll be calling for me today sometime."

"That's...illegal. And your message privileges won't last long."

"I suppose not, once they find I'm a fraud."

"I'll lend you one of mine."

She took back the paper and wrote a new message-ID and a password.

"You're a kind and generous person."

"So are you. You realize that by allowing me to film our talk, you've made me very rich."

"Really?"

"The success of my show depends on ratings. My salary depends on those ratings. You've given me a world exclusive. Thank you."

"You're welcome, Madhar Nect. Can I impose upon you further? It would help if I had a proper computer interface to your networks."

She laughed, "I could probably be shot for giving our technology to an alien!"

"I'll bring it back."

Madhar took Jim into the house again and loaded him up with some surprisingly sophisticated equipment.

As Jim was about to climb aboard the flier to leave, he noticed Madhar was looking over his flier once more.

She mused, "We used chemical rockets for our first spaceships."

Jim froze. "What did you say?"

"For our first spaceships, they had highly explosive propellant."

"What spaceships? I thought you weren't interested in space travel."

"It was a long time ago."

"Wh-what happened?"

"Well, you know, it's a rather long story," she looked at Jim's ship from front to back and front again, "but it's one I'm particularly saddened by."

"Please, go on."

"The governing alliance of the day boasted that they could put people on Mainworld. It was a political thing. They thought they could keep the alliance going if there was a Great Work to focus everybody's attention. So they did it: they built the ships; proved the technology; sent some brave boys into orbit, then into orbit around Mainworld; and, finally, they landed there."

She paused and sighed. "When the Regdenir found out, they were furious. They had assumed it wasn't possible, so they had done nothing to stop the program. But once it happened, then the storm came. They traded influence, enough to bring the alliance down. They cut off vital power supplies for several days. They made sure that no one went back. They killed the space organization by starving it of funds and people. For them, you see, it was sacrilegious to touch Mainworld. Of course, in those days, we thought we might be the only sentient life in the universe." Madhar looked into Jim's eyes and said quietly, "We could have been out there with you all by now."

"Maybe they think differently now. Now one of them has been out and about?"

"Tree-climbers! Save us from tree-climbers!"

<hr>

wehorulanVjiirVregde4Vapp

Greetings, Wehorulan Jiir.

I am a friend of Madhar Nect, with whom you corresponded some time ago.

I am in need of your help.

I wish to correspond with a Barottin Regdenir who has used the name "Edward."

He has recently purchased some advanced scientific equipment.

I do not represent any government agency. I am not investigating any crime.

I hope you can be of help.

g101VnectVlatsinVux

---

g101VnectVlatsinVux

It is not our practice to enter open-ended correspondence with others.

In return for the willingness to help me shown by Madhar Nect, I offer this.

For a period of eight days you may access our message system with this ID:

aaaaVjiirVregde99Vapp

First password aaaa

Begin at regde99Vaudnir.

You will find it has limited access, but it may be sufficient for your search.

Rest in Beauty.

wehorulanVjiirVregde4Vapp

Jim sighed as he read the message. He doubted this would be any good.

He had again taken up his position above Mainworld. The TV prattled on in the background. He had tried to find a documentary about the Regdenir, as Madhar had suggested. Nothing had been broadcast during the External Intelligence Agency's monitoring, nor during the week since he had arrived.

He looked again at the message. He thought "regde99" was perhaps the outermost layer of the Regdenir world. "Audnir" was more interesting from a linguistic point of view. The suffix "nir" looked like it had to do with a group or membership. "Aud," he remembered, was a word for the out-of-doors, the countryside, or a remote region. Perhaps it also indicated non-Regde.

He decided the location *audnir* must be the interface for all external interaction. Had Edward been asking for any help from audnirs like Madhar Nect? There was only one way to find out.

Jim slowly began his journey into the world of the Regdenir.

All things are related.

If you find a hierarchy, such as Negge, who is father to Haro and Johe, who is father to Bet and Megga, be sure of this: there are relationships that exist only between Negge and Bet, between Haro and Bet, between Megga and Negge; different relationships exist between Haro and Johe other than kinship, and between Megga and Bet, the same. You can never see the hierarchy but in its incompleteness.

In a world interwoven and fluid, something must be absolute. There must be one fundamental root of all. As the arra worm is rooted to the rock so that the b'arra fish can eat its extrusions, so we need to feed on that which is absolute. This fundamental root we know as Beauty.

Jim learned these things from his first few trips into the Regde message areas. His head hurt. His back hurt. His stomach still ached from breakfasting on blancar. What he really wanted was to go home.

He found lists of names, but "Edward" was not in them. He found lists of documents, but none had any bearing on his business as far as he could tell. He found lists of further places to look, but was there a point? The Regde were loquacious. It seemed they wrote down everything. Jim felt like an ant crawling over the crumbs at the bottom of the first pile, at the edge of the first mound, at the bottom of the first foothill of a range of mountains.

He switched off his link and lowered the seatback and the lights. Sleep, however, was not so easy to arrange.

In his troubled state, Jim remembered how straightforward this was going to be: a simple job to bring him back into active service. His mind wandered to his suspension. From there, it was a short step back into the pit.

The craft took off. He knew the pilot. He knew all about him.

The craft turned, weapons firing.

The police flier erupted in flames.

The craft turned again. People began to move away from the windows of the terminal.

Useless panic.

The glass whispered open, and the rockets coughed into the marble floor.

Then the nightmare began.

The smoke and rubble.

The bodies.

The unrecognizable pieces.

The groans.

The hopeless last breaths.

And then the guilt.

Jim woke up with his tears soaking the headrest.

He showered and returned to the pilot's seat. He looked out the windows down onto Turcanis Major V and its two moons, both visible beyond. He looked out farther into the darkness.

Someone, he had read, once asked Albert Einstein what he thought was the greatest unsolved mystery. "Is the universe friendly?" was the great man's reply.

That was before humanity had made contact with other worlds, before it had learned the techniques of long-distance travel and taken its place in the galaxy-wide trading culture.

Right now, Jim thought in his loneliness, *we still don't know.*

He linked into the Regdenir system again. This time he looked again at the helpful hints for newcomers. He wanted to find something like the children's TV shows that had been so useful before.

Within ten minutes he had found it. There was a message board. Anyone could write to it; anyone could answer. It was a place for children to ask questions about scripture and have the best teachers reply. Jim spent an hour browsing messages and answers. Several replies came from Regde1 IDs.

Some message lines were hot debates with many writers quoting from what Jim guessed was their scripture. The scriptural language was challenging, quite different from the modern speech used in the television programs and from the dialect of Madhar Nect. Other lines were tedious arguments over the nuanced definitions of individual words or phrases. One, he was amused to see, was over whether it was proper to pause for breath before or after a particular word when reciting one part of scripture.

Jim composed his question with care.

misquuerVappquuerVregde99Vapp
Greetings.

I wish to correspond with any who have knowledge of other worlds or technology that might come from other worlds.

Has anyone such knowledge?
aaaaVjiirVregde99Vapp

A reply came quickly.

misquuerVappquuerVregde99Vapp

Greetings, guest of Jiir.

We do not seek the ways of audnir.

The ways of Regdenir are our strength.

If such knowledge comes to us, we may use it.

To seek it is not our way.

Rest in Beauty.

mardrewVlartuVregde1Vapp

A reply to the reply came soon after.

misquuerVappquuerVregde99Vapp

Greetings, guest of Jiir.

If the way of Beauty is served by such knowledge, it is not forbidden.

The generation of electricity from the tides was not our knowledge at first. We took it and transformed it into the service of Beauty.

Maybe we can do so also to the knowledge of aud-audnir.

angaraVmyournVregde1Vapp

Then came another.

misquuerVappquuerVregde99Vapp

Greetings, guest of Jiir.

There is only audnir. To differentiate between the origins of audnir is to disguise the necessary truth.

That which is not born of Beauty cannot be looked to, to find Beauty.

clostuVbarnezVregde2Vmib

Jim watched in wonder as the messages added to each other.

---

misquuerVappquuerVregde99Vapp

Greetings, guest of Jiir.

Perhaps Clostu Barnez is correct.

Then when we saw the Beauty in the tides, we should have been content.

Did we not look to the audnir for the technology for generators?

It was not from the Beauty we had, but it is part of the Beauty we have now.

Is this not wondrous? That Beauty can come to us, even from unlikely places?

angaraVmyournVregde1Vapp

---

misquuerVappquuerVregde99Vapp

Greetings, guest of Jiir.

Perhaps Angara Myourn is correct.

Then Beauty is to be found in all the people of all the worlds.

Then there is no audnir; there is no Regdenir. Only Beauty spread so thinly on the dust of space none can tell it from dirt!

If we need the machines of audnir, why are we different?

Rest in Beauty.

mardrewVlartuVregde1Vapp

---

misquuerVappquuerVregde99Vapp

Greetings, guest of Jiir.

Perhaps the esteemed Mardrew Lartu is correct, and I am corrected.

Then if we take the machines of audnir, we are the same as audnir.

Unless, of course, our ways with these machines are different.

Unless, of course, our thoughts about them are different.

Unless, of course, our desires are different.

Unless, of course, we know Beauty.

And in that Beauty, we can make the things that are not Beauty, because of their origins, into Beauty, because of their use.

angaraVmyournVregde1Vapp

▭

There were more lines of conversation in a similar vein. One message, in the midst of the minor storm he had started, almost went unnoticed.

▭

misquuerVappquuerVregde99Vapp

Greetings, guest of Jiir.

I have come to think that any audnir machines that can enhance our appreciation of Beauty are not only permissible but should be actively sought out.

The reason for our very being is to worship Beauty. Anything that enhances our worship can be brought in from the outside.

dlaviVherucVregde3Vopp

▭

Two things struck Jim about the message: one was the open sentiment; the other was something he remembered. Madhar had said they worshiped Mainworld. Dlavi said they worshiped Beauty.

Were they the same thing? He felt this was important. *Who can I ask without seeming a complete idiot?*

A quick message to Madhar brought the answer.

---

aaaaVjiirVregde99Vapp

Greetings, Jim Able.

I knew you would find your way in.

Yes, they worship Mainworld. They refer to it always as Beauty.

If you can find out how an otherwise rational section of our population can do this, let me know.

You'll be a television sensation in three days' time.

madharVnectVlatsinVux

Time for a leap of faith, Jim thought.

---

dlaviVherucVregde3Vopp

Greetings, Dlavi Heruc.

I am from a curious people.

We wonder how an infrared scanner can help the worship of Beauty.

I earnestly wish to meet with you, solely to gather some information.

aaaaVjiirVregde99Vapp

It was several hours before the reply came.

---

aaaaVjiirVregde99Vapp

Greetings, guest of Jiir, of a curious people.

I know little of these matters. I have other concerns than these.

This I know. My friend is a holy and good person.

This I know. He will be glad to give you all the information you require.

This I know. I have but one part of the audnir device installed in the roof of my house.

This I know. My friend has assured me no heresy hides in its shadow.

You may find him at sophaVlucaVregde3Vopp.

May you and your people rest in Beauty.

dlaviVherucVregde3Vopp

⬜

"When a direct shot doesn't connect, a ricochet will do," Jim spoke to the screen, sighing with relief. He brought out the communication prepared for the occasion by Liz Curacao.

⬜

sophaVlucaVregde3Vopp

Greetings, Sopha Luca.

Greetings, Edward of Turcanis.

I wish to consult with you.

When a people who have no dealings with others undertakes a trade, it is in the interests of all parties for the circumstances to be clearly defined.

Did the trade represent one of a future series of trades?

Was the trade an unhappy experience that the trader does not wish to repeat?

The suppliers of the goods may be in a position to advise, both on its use and on the use of other devices, which may, as yet, be unknown to the buyer. Devices, perhaps, that can assist the buyer in his religious practices and observances.

I am not a trader myself but rather an officer of information. I am not a police officer, nor has any crime been committed.

I wish to meet with you to discuss these matters. Please consider this request in the spirit of open friendship in which it is offered.

aaaaVjiirVregde99Vapp

———

Jim liked the religious part, which was his own improvisation.

It was a day—a long day—of waiting before the reply came.

CHAPTER FOUR

---

aaaaVjiirVregde99Vapp

Greetings, traveler.

I am impressed by your investigative success.

I have no need for more information, nor trade, nor advice, nor another device, nor contact.

I do not think you know enough of our religious practices and observances to have any basis for further discussion.

sophaVlucaVregde3Vopp

"Bastard!" muttered Jim as he read.

---

sophaVlucaVregde3Vopp

Greetings, Sopha Luca.

Perhaps I was not clear in my previous message.

I request a meeting. A short meeting. At this meeting I wish to discuss with you the future of relations between the people of your world and the people of the wider galaxy.

You have become, intentionally or otherwise, the first ambassador from your planet.

aaaaVjiirVregde99Vapp

---

aaaaVjiirVregde99Vapp

Greetings, traveler.

Your first message was clear.

There will be no further contact between the people of this planet and the people of the wider galaxy.

There will be no meeting between us.

sophaVlucaVregde3Vopp

Jim felt his mission slipping away from him. How could he have come so far and be met with such blanket resistance?

He drafted several angry replies—and erased them all. He stared at the picture of Sopha. He tried to imagine the blue-cloaked figure writing these messages. He tried to imagine what else Sopha was doing. What were their religious practices? How did they worship a planet?

"Damn you for being right!" Jim said to the picture.

---

sophaVlucaVregde3Vopp

Greetings, Sopha Luca.

I have meditated upon your replies and our current situation.

You are correct; I know little of your ways.

I know the Regdenir are a serious and thoughtful people. I doubt you made your purchase on a whim.

I will leave your system shortly and perhaps never return.

I understand from my contact among your audnir cousins that images of me will soon appear on their television system. I was interviewed by a scientist. The interview will be transmitted, I think, tomorrow.

Perhaps this will bring about a renewal of interest in space travel among them.

Perhaps the people of your world may yet explore their own system and then explore, with us, the rest of the galaxy.

My name is James Able. I work for Sol Earth's Office of External Affairs in the Department of Extra-Solar Activities.

Please contact me there if you ever need to.

I have one last question. Why do you call your main planet "Beauty"?

aaaaVjiirVregde99Vapp

---

aaaaVjiirVregde99Vapp

Greetings, James Able.

Then you are from Earth. I met several of your race and found them to be reasonable people.

Is it in your power to prevent the transmission of which you write?

sophaVlucaVregde3Vopp

---

sophaVlucaVregde3Vopp

Greetings, Sopha Luca.

Why would I wish to do that?

aaaaVjiirVregde99Vapp

---

aaaaVjiirVregde99Vapp

Greetings, James Able.
Prevent the transmission and I agree to meet with you.
sophaVlucaVregde3Vopp

---

madharVnectVlatsinVux
Greetings, Madhar Nect.
I have traced Edward. He has refused to meet me unless your show with me is canceled or at least postponed.
Please acknowledge.
From Jim Able
aaaaVjiirVregde99Vapp

---

aaaaVjiirVregde99Vapp
Greetings, Jim Able.
Congratulations on your detective work.
No way.
madharVnectVlatsinVux

---

madharVnectVlatsinVux
Greetings, Madhar Nect.
Perhaps you are correct, and I gave you full rights to broadcast my words and image at any time for your own profit.
Then I must ask this question: how long does it take to repair a satellite network when there has been damage from collisions with another orbiting object?
From Jim Able
aaaaVjiirVregde99Vapp

---

aaaaVjiirVregde99Vapp

Greetings, Jim Able.

You write like a Barottin Regdenir of the first order and bargain like one too!

In our culture, Jim Able, it is a violation of friendship when a guest threatens the host who has shared her food!

How long a postponement do you need? I have already done the advance publicity. The longer the delay, the more of a tree-climber I appear.

madharVnectVlatsinVux

---

madharVnectVlatsinVux

Greetings, Madhar Nect.

I need only as long as it takes for my meeting with Edward. I would guess two days extra.

From Jim Able

aaaaVjiirVregde99Vapp

---

aaaaVjiirVregde99Vapp

Greetings, Jim Able.

Two days. Agreed.

Restore our friendship by recording a further session with me before you leave. There are many questions I now wish I had asked you.

madharVnectVlatsinVux

So far, so good, thought Jim.

---

sophaVlucaVregde3Vopp

Greetings, Sopha Luca.

I have secured the transmission.

Please send details of where we can meet in private. I presume you do not wish me to be seen by others.

aaaaVjiirVregde99Vapp

---

aaaaVjiirVregde99Vapp

Greetings, James Able.

I live in the city of Oppudim.

To the north of the city is an area of forest.

In the valley that lies to the east between the two tallest mountains is where I land and keep my craft. It is secluded enough for our purposes.

There is a retreat house there; you will be comfortably accommodated.

Be sure you arrive during daylight. This is important if you are to be undetected. Do not arrive after dark!

I will go there now and prepare. If I can, I will activate a beacon for you to follow.

sophaVlucaVregde3Vopp

Jim lay back and congratulated himself on having solved the problem. He had successfully pushed a hot button with the Regdenir. Edward, or rather, Sopha, was going to meet him.

Let's hope Sopha isn't so worried by the broadcast that he tries anything foolish, he thought.

Somewhere at the back of his mind was a note he had written when Liz was lecturing him.

"Don't start a war," she had said.

"Relax," he'd replied, "nothing can go wrong."

Jim timed his journey so that he would arrive just after midday. He came in on the steepest path he could persuade his craft to perform. He hoped to be as close to the sun's position in the sky as he could. He thought it odd that Sopha had insisted on a daytime landing rather than coming in under the cover of night.

Oppudim was a compact city. The area of forest to its north was enormous. Jim scanned the valley Sopha had mentioned. It was long and flat, but its sides were steep. It stretched a long way to the east from the mountains. It was a perfect place to hide a flier. The valley walls would shield a takeoff from all but the people in the valley itself.

Jim approached it from the south and dropped over the valley wall several miles from the mountains. Immediately after he entered the valley, the beacon was audible on a standard frequency.

He slowed the craft and headed up the valley. He wondered if its dense trees might be covering a huge population or paths no Turcanian had ever trod. This, perhaps, was the middle of nowhere; from the air, there was no way of telling.

A landing strip came into view, stretching down a cleared area below a couple of low buildings. He landed and then rolled the flier to a halt at the top of the strip. He waited for his craft to cool a little before opening the hatch. No one had yet appeared to greet him.

The first thing that Jim became aware of was the humidity. The air was thick and heavy. It was laden with a strong smell of mold. He coughed involuntarily, and it was a minute or so before he got his breath back.

"James Able."

He looked down at the blue-cloaked figure standing regally at the foot of the ramp.

"Edward? I mean, Sopha?"

The figure bowed and, turning, began to walk toward the nearer building.

Jim paused to secure his craft and followed, already sweating with the simple exertion of walking. The songs of thousands of birds filled the spaces under the trees. The forest throbbed with noises. At the edge of Jim's vision, what looked like insects flicked through the air, twinkling in the sunlight. The trees themselves were a type Jim had not yet seen on this world, quite different from those around the quiet bay at Martorn. They had thick and leafy canopies, mottled white branches, and high skirts of roots looping and spreading around the lower half of the trunks like mangroves.

The building was a single story with wide windows, giving a view of the long landing strip and of the lower parts of the forest. It seemed to be made of the local rock, similar in color to the mountains' peaks and the ragged edge of the valley wall above. The smaller building behind it, he could now see, was a wide, low wooden structure.

Sopha led Jim through an opening near one corner of the main building into a spacious stone-floored chamber. The sound of gently falling water calmed the more raucous voices of the forest. To Jim's initial alarm, the water rose from the floor in the center of the room. It began as a column no higher than twelve inches, spreading in a circle some twenty feet across, to disappear through an expertly hidden cut in the stone. The dark shine of the stone was so like the surface of the water that it seemed the whole floor was liquid and that it was pouring itself out from the center.

Jim followed Sopha around the fountain and through a wide doorway into a small room. Here there were several seats arranged before a small platform. Sopha sat on an ornate chair on the platform. He gestured for Jim to sit on one of the seats below him.

This is not a meeting of equals, Jim thought, *but I can wait.*

"Would you like some refreshments?"

Jim nodded. "Sure."

He thought, *What was it Madhar said about sharing food?*

Sopha clapped his hands, and three blue-cloaked figures appeared with their hoods up, obscuring their faces. With lightning efficiency and precision, they arranged a small table next to him. On it was a cup, a jug of cold brown liquid, and several small plates of unfamiliar food.

"Thank you very much," Jim said, trying to catch the eye of one of the servers.

"They will not speak. These are three of my sons. They are in training at the moment and are restricted in their activities."

"Oh, do you have a large family?"

"I am blessed with fourteen offspring."

"Ah. Congratulations."

"And you?"

"No. I have no family. I'm not married."

Sopha said nothing but nodded and continued to gaze fixedly on his face as, Jim realized, he had been doing since they sat down.

Sopha began to speak in Standard as Jim sipped the drink. "Let us review why you have come to me. You come from a race whose joy is in exploration. You actively seek other races. You relish trade and exchange. 'Perhaps,' you say to yourselves, 'this Turcanian race will trade with us?' Then you seek me, for you know I have traveled. Then you send messages to me, hoping to continue such dealings."

"That's a fair summary. We wish to learn about you. We mean you no harm. I was to contact your government first, to ask for permission and for help. Madhar Nect explained something of your world's politics to me. And so I found you by myself. When I began, I did not know of the—shall I say—differences between the Regdenir and the audnir."

"It is sad that you first went to the blind to ask what they see."

"I don't understand."

"No, James Able, you do not. That is why I have met with you. I will teach you. I will show you the truth of this matter so you may go back to Earth and trouble us no more. You are ignorant of our ways, through no choice of yours, but you have been in the company of those whose ignorance is by choice. Did you visit Madhar Nect by day or night?"

"I arrived after dark and left early in the morning."

"And let me tell you what she did. She took you inside her dwelling. She fed you and talked to you, but at no time did she open a window or look out of her door. All night. Is this correct?"

"I—I suppose so. Is that important?"

"I will teach you. The audnir are pitiable creatures. They have blinded themselves and wander lost. They claim to seek knowledge. They proclaim their 'science.' They extol their politics and studies of society and psychology. Perhaps they are right, and darkness and confusion are the fate of all creatures. The Regdenir stand against their ignorance."

"I'm not following you at all."

"No, but you will. I will answer the question you asked me. We must both prepare for this evening."

"Prepare for what this evening?"

"No. Prepare for this evening. You wish to know of our religious observances. Tonight, you will join me in our main worship. You will be the first person from another world to witness such things. Tonight, I will teach you."

Jim let this news sink in for a moment.

"I am honored. What will I have to do?"

"You will have to open your eyes and your ears. You will bring your mind, the mind that successfully solved the puzzle of my identity, to bear on more weighty matters. You will have to see where you have thought yourself blind."

Jim said nothing.

"For the remainder of the daylight hours, I must return to my work. Join me that you may see the achievements of the Regdenir."

Jim allowed himself a moment of satisfaction. He had found Edward and overcome the Regdenir's initial refusal to meet. He had been welcomed as a guest. He would witness a religious ritual, which perhaps the rest of the Turcanian population had never seen. *So far, so good, and not at all bad,* he thought, *for a first job back from medical leave.*

Sopha led Jim back through the fountain room and through a small door.

They were in a room about thirty feet square. It had no windows. Along three of the walls were computer consoles. One wall had a grid of twelve monitors. Beneath the grid were one keyboard and several other small devices.

"From here we can access the recorded wisdom of the Regdenir. This is our work. This is trade. This is our exploration, James Able."

"Nect said you had your Holy Scriptures in a database."

"At the core of what you will see are the words of scripture, yes. All our efforts are in the study and exploration of the truths within them. The language of the old times is difficult. I doubt that your training will have prepared you for it."

"No, from what I saw in the Regde99 message area, it didn't."

"Would it surprise you to know that most Regdenir do not understand it either?"

"I—yes. Don't you study it?"

"Most only study the main translations, the commentaries, the discussions, and the analyses. It is sad that our young do not delve deeper. Such are the times we live in."

Sopha took his seat under the large grid of monitors. Jim watched as one by one they came to life. Sopha was joining in on twelve concurrent conversations, much like the one Jim had started in Regde99. He switched from screen to screen fluidly, adding a message and moving on. As he worked, the lists of messages were constantly refreshing as other correspondents weighed in on each topic.

"Forgive me a moment, James Able. I must catch up on certain matters. I will explain more to you shortly."

"That's okay, if you don't mind my watching."

Sopha said nothing, returning his attention to a lengthy contribution on the upper left screen, which seemed to center on the disputed definition of an archaic word.

After an hour of waiting and watching, Jim had learned a few things about the computer setup. He saw that the screens along the side walls were linked to various lower levels within the Regdenir world. The grid was devoted to Regde3, which Jim knew from his message address was Sopha's level. Near the door, he found one machine that was linked to a database in the Deneb system. In a folder lying on the table nearby, he found a picture of himself, the details of his position in the OEA, and a printed copy of the message to Sopha where he had given him his name.

Without turning to see what Jim was up to, Sopha began to speak.

"This computer system is called the Regdekol. Do you understand the word?"

"Regde-kol," Jim repeated. "Yes, 'kol' means 'sculpture.'"

"Almost. It means both sculpture and architecture. It means the artistic creative process and the care with which the brush is applied to the canvas. It means both to create with steady skill and to control the growth of a living organism. Do you understand?"

"I think so."

"Its founding minds laid down the rock—the Holy Works. Each generation that has followed has built upon this foundation. We see the holy words and the blessed commentaries of our greatest minds through the years, dissecting, expanding, enlivening, and...What is the word for 'mikfasal'?"

"Umm, 'midwife'?"

"Yes, being midwife to the birth of new meaning." Sopha's voice showed an excitement that Jim had not heard in it before.

"Each commentary is also studied. The works of the scholars wrap around them like the ornamentation on a pot. The learning of each new generation increases the total of our knowledge. Do you understand?"

"Sure."

"Your audnir scientist might put it like this. The Holy Scripture is the first dimension. The commentaries of the teachers are the second dimension."

"Okay," said Jim, without quite meaning it.

"Now what you see here," he said, gesturing to the grid and the rest of the room, "these are the third dimension. Every teaching has ideas common to other teachings. To find the commonality, you would have to search through each two-dimensional entry, yes? We have built the Regdekol to follow the three dimensions of truth through all the commentaries, all the learning, all the discussion and study. All the relationships are here."

He looked at Jim, his eyes bright in the shadow of his overhanging brows.

"For us, divine truth is a three-dimensional thing. Each contribution, each contributor, brings an expression of interlinked truths. We can see the links in each other's thoughts. We can follow the routes of study of hundreds of fellow minds as we explore deeper and deeper into those truths."

Jim looked at the message lists, growing and splitting before his widening eyes. "You can cross-reference everything you write?"

"Better yet, we can, as you say, 'cross-reference' the *ideas* we contribute across the whole of the Regdekol. When I said to you this was the recorded wisdom of the Regdenir, you perhaps thought I meant it to be some sort of library of documents, yes?"

Jim nodded.

"It is far more."

"How can your mind cope with it all? I knew already that you did things in a meticulous way. But—such a broad scale—all that detail? You were splitting your concentration across twelve different topics."

"'The effective mind is a trained mind,' as I tell my sons. But surely in your work you must deal with many small details at once?"

"What about things that you don't agree with?" Jim asked, "There must be ideas that you don't go along with."

Sopha hesitated. "There are times when an idea is deemed heretical. The great teachers who, you see, are Regdel, they can so"—he paused—"wrap around an idea, in all its referents, such that only they can see it. They can 'encapsulate' perhaps, or 'seal it off,' yes? But even then, their commentaries upon it may become the bedrock of new learning and new layers of thought."

Jim began to reply, but something Sopha had said had started a chain reaction in him: his job was based on details. He was constantly trying to be meticulous, as scrupulous with details as Sopha seemed to be. He was suddenly overtaken by a memory of the detail he had missed.

It was to do with a human, one not born on Earth. He was working as a courier for a couple of the larger bulk shippers. The first time Jim interviewed him was to check on a forged security clearance that had turned up in a burned-out flier. The fellow had complained about signing any physical forms. He had a real aversion to committing his written signature to anything. He wanted everything to be done electronically.

The second interview was at a pleasant Sin Har spaceport called Ch'Garratt. That was a routine check. It was just a matter of going through his logbook and cross-checking it against the filings received at the OEA.

It was his watch—a simple wristwatch. At the first interview, he had worn it with the face slung inward under his wrist rather than by the back of his hand. It was on his right hand.

The second interview had taken place many months after the first. The man had signed the printed list of variances without a word of complaint. The watch was on his left wrist.

Over the course of nearly a year, the image of the watch had become clearer and clearer. Jim could count the hairs on the man's wrist, sticking up around the strap of the watch.

But he hadn't noticed then. He wasn't suspicious enough when it counted.

Somehow he had known it wasn't the same guy. Somehow he had seen the change in attitude. He had seen the wristwatch, but when a mental alarm should have sounded, Jim had had no reaction.

The police flier had taken off almost at the same time as the courier's ship.

Whoever he was, he panicked.

He fired a missile and brought the police vehicle down and, then, came after Jim. He leveled the terminal building and flew off.

Nearly a hundred people had died and as many were seriously injured. Jim had pulled several of them out of the wreckage with his own burnt hands.

. . .

It was a small detail that became a ten-month suspension from duty.

It was a recurrent nightmare that six months of counseling had not quieted.

Sopha was talking to him. He felt the rough skin of the Turcanian's hand on the side of his head.

"James Able, are you unwell?"

"Huh? I'm fine."

"There is something wrong, I think. You have, if not a sickness of body, a sickness of spirit!"

"No, it's okay. It's just that something you said triggered a-an unpleasant memory."

Sopha continued to hold Jim by the side of his head and peer into his eyes. "I do not know enough about your race to know the way to treat sickness. But come here to the next room and sit awhile."

He led Jim back to the fountain room and lowered him into a chair facing the dark expanse of the water. Jim's host sat next to him and remained silent for several minutes.

"Tell me your memory."

Jim thought for a moment, wondering if he should take this strange alien into his confidence. He felt disorientated, perhaps by the humidity, perhaps by the shock of finding the Regdenir not quite as ridiculous as Madhar had led him to expect. He knew he needed to regain control of this encounter, to get the information he needed, and leave. But it was too late. His rational mind was in suspension; his feelings had taken over.

"It was a small detail...and many people died."

He told Sopha the whole story. At the end, he felt tired and sad. Sopha did not immediately make any comment.

"Do as I do," he said quietly.

He got up and knelt at the edge of the water, his knees close to the edge of the floor where the shallow flow disappeared under the precisely cut tiling.

Jim did the same, feeling extremely self-conscious.

Sopha leaned forward and placed his hands flat on the stone underneath the flowing water. Jim followed and was surprised to find the water was chilled.

"Look at your reflection in the water."

Jim looked and saw himself looking pale and shadowy.

"Now, take some water and wash it over your face."

Sopha scooped up some water and allowed a small trickle to run over his bumpy head. Jim scooped a handful and let it drip into his hair.

"Our prayer for this translates to 'Let this wash my darkness away.' It is necessary for all to come here from time to time. There is nothing shameful in it."

Jim nodded. They got up, and Sopha led the way through the classroom, where they had begun their meeting, into a large kitchen. Immediately his sons were in attendance. Sopha gave a few commands, and the three obeyed without uttering a word in reply.

This time, Sopha also took the drink provided. Jim enjoyed it, despite its green color and vinegary smell.

"Soon we shall begin our evening worship," said Sopha. "I ask you to wait with your questions until then."

Jim answered, "Okay, but tell me one thing in case I forget to ask you. Why did you call yourself 'Edward' rather than 'Sopha'?"

Sopha smiled and sipped his drink.

"When I was first learning your language and mastering the techniques to interface with your computers, I found a database of names. I think it was intended for those expecting new offspring. In it, I found the name 'Edward' and a description. It said that it was a name associated with royalty, which the Regdenir consider themselves. It gave a meaning for the name as 'a rich or powerful guardian.' This also the Regdenir consider themselves. We are guardians of the truth. It amused me to use the name in dealing with the strangers I met."

"I see. And also allowed you some anonymity, making you difficult to trace."

"Apparently not." He smiled again.

When they had finished their drinks, they got up and returned to the fountain room.

"Please wait here while we prepare. The daylight will end in an hour. We must walk up to the promontory above the house before then."

The journey to the promontory left Jim gasping for breath and covered in sweat. The path up the rise behind the retreat house was a series of precipitous switchbacks that the Regdenir negotiated with an ease that Jim could not match. He pushed past overgrown ferns and pumped his legs up the slopes but fell behind at every turn.

Ahead of him, Sopha led his three sons and two other Regdenir Jim had not seen before. He wondered as he climbed if they had been deliberately kept hidden. He guessed Sopha was a good enough strategist to have a backup plan in case his meeting with an unknown alien had not gone well.

Around the last bend, the path leveled out and led into a narrow tunnel of interwoven branches and hanging leaves. Rushing through the arch at its far end, Jim skidded to a halt, suddenly in the open and blinking in the light. He saw the Regdenir some way ahead of him, standing in a line and bowing, hoods hiding their faces. The ceremony was already underway.

Jim felt disappointed that he was, apparently, not invited to participate, nor given any explanation of what was taking place. He was allowed to attend and otherwise forgotten.

He stood where he was, taking stock of what he could see. The tunnel had led to a circular stone platform, perhaps six hundred feet in diameter. Only the figures of the Regdenir interrupted its flat expanse. There was neither edging nor railing to hide the view of the valley beyond. At his feet were intricate etchings in the black stone. His eyes followed long curved lines connected with others in a continuous work that seemed to cover the entire surface.

The sun was setting behind the two mountain peaks to Jim's left. He was glad to be in time to see the bare rock glow with the fiery backlight. He continued to watch for a while, until it struck him that the others were all facing east. He had a momentary flush of embarrassment, fearing he had already missed something important, but the Regdenir had not moved.

He could hear Sopha's voice lifted in prayer alternating with the others' chanted responses; the language was not the Turcanian of common speech. He had hoped to follow the ceremony, to learn from it, but he could understand nothing of what was being said or sung.

The sounds of the forest faded as soon as the sun had set. Distant hissing and whistling noises rose from beyond the platform. The noise grew into the unmistakable sound of rushing water. Jim remembered Madhar's description of the underground cisterns pouring their contents into the valleys and marshes to power the Regdenir electric grid. He understood the awesome scale of the tides when the sound of the water became a deep rumble that sent up a steady vibration through the platform.

As the night sky darkened, the Regdenir continued their prayers. Jim thought to go out into the middle of the platform and join them, but his feeling of being the forgotten guest held him back. He moved slowly over to the edge of the platform at his right and carefully looked down. He could see the wall of the valley falling away into the shadows below.

The Regdenir fell silent. All but Sopha knelt on the stone and bowed their heads. In the deepening darkness, they seemed to Jim to become a tableau carved from the black rock around them. It stirred a memory of the Christmas nativity scenes of his youth. Now, Jim noticed a green tinge on the eastern horizon.

Back across the platform, a similar glow reflected from the tops of the mountains. As he watched, it spread lower and lower down the mountainside.

The moment the green dawn lit Sopha's face, the Regdenir spoke a single word, the others began to sing, and to Jim's lasting astonishment, Turcanis Major V burst over the horizon.

THE FILE

Office of External Affairs
Department of Extra-Solar Activities

CONFIDENTIAL

C1 – 032 – TURCANIS MAJOR – Techno-transfer

Assigned to: James Able

Introduction Form – FC01

Reported: *August 4, 2198*

Claimant Name (original): | *Yacov Barnu*

Claimant Name (phonetic, if required):

Describe yourself:

I run a store on Arietis Station 156.
My business is small-scale electronics, for entertainment purposes.

Describe the nature of the First Contact:

During May 2198 I opened my door to a customer whose race I did not
recognize. I attach a video capture as supporting evidence.
After discussing his request for high-end scanning equipment, I asked him
to identify his home world. He seemed unused to standard astro-charting.
With some difficulty we established he came from Turcanis Major V-1
(Five-one).
I asked how he knew Standard. He told me he had monitored transmissions
from survey vessels working his sector.
I did not understand his occupation. He was either an author or a priest.
He seemed both intelligent and naïve.

Declaration:

I believe myself to be the first person to introduce this new race to the Earth and claim all fees and rewards previously published in pursuance of this introduction.

I give my signature to this document in affirmation of all its contents:

Sign here: | **Y BARNU**

Note: This form may only be used for First Contact Claims for the introduction fees current at time of signature. For details of current fees contact issuing authority. DO NOT USE THIS FORM for any other claims as this will delay processing.

For Office use only

Authorized for payment

Date: *September 13, 2198*

By the authority of the Secretary of the Office of Expansion Services

Mdme. Cheri Busca

Assistant to the Secretary

Memo August 21, 2198
Officer Shane Golder

Re: First Contact Report - Yacov Barnu

Arietis Station is a Hamalan colony, mixed race.
The attached in-store security video capture shows the person in question but the quality is poor.

I have received twenty-five First Contact reports from Mr. Barnu. It seems that whenever regular business is slack, strange new races rush into his store.
Even if this is the exception that proves the rule I have two other concerns resulting from the limited information Mr. Barnu has provided.

a)   How did the alien arrive? If he came with another race, the claim is theirs. If he came in his own craft, why has no encounter happened before? If ships are leaving TMV-I for trade, someone should have seen them before now.

b)   If they can build their own ships, why would he wish to buy something as simple as scanning equipment?

I recommend this claim be placed in suspension pending further contact.
SG

General Briefing
5478

All ship captains, colony heads,
base commanders, and station managers
are hereby henceforth required to

Report all sightings and contacts with residents
of any planet in the **Turcanis Major system**.

A Video Capture is attached.

It is NOT considered that the inhabitants
of the aforesaid system are dangerous
or suspected of any criminal activity.
This requirement is for
INFORMATIONAL PURPOSES ONLY
at this time.

This order is enforced upon the authority of

Elizabeth Curacao
Assistant to the Secretary
Office of External Affairs
Department of Extra-Solar Activities
September 13, 2198

Introduction Form – FC01

Reported: **December 29, 2198**

Claimant Name (original): **Michlev Apporto Nmathe Pharano**

Claimant Name (phonetic, if required):

Describe yourself:

I captain a supply ship for the Himdu-Cola Company based on Callistri.

Describe the nature of the First Contact:

On Mustur 8 5600 we were in orbit around a customer's planet.

(Approx May, 2198/name withheld)

The pilot of a small craft hailed us. I did not recognize his race.

(scanner matrix attached)

He requested trade for advanced scanning equipment.

(communications log capture attached)

He identified his home world only as Turcanis Major.

(probably TM Five-One)

I was unable to assist him with this particular trade but gave him my contact information and offered my services to continue his relationship with Earth.

Declaration:

I believe myself to be the first person to introduce this new race to the Earth and claim all fees and rewards previously published in pursuance of this introduction.

I give my signature to this document in affirmation of all its contents:

Sign here: MICHLEV Ap/Nm/Ph/ZDS Himdu-Cola

Note: This form may only be used for First Contact Claims for the introduction fees current at time of signature. For details of current fees contact issuing authority. DO NOT USE THIS FORM for any other claims as this will delay processing.

For Office use only
Authorized for payment

Date:

By the authority of the Secretary of the Office of Expansion Services

Assistant to the Secretary

[Received January 5, 2199 O4#JD-8989]

From: Colonel M. Staffar, DF25

To: Elizabeth Curacao, OEA

January 5, 2199

Dear Elizabeth,

In response to GB5478 I can offer this, alas secondhand, account of a Turcanian.

Between October 5 and October 13, 2198 my crews had several reports of a small vessel working around the station. Each had been hailed en route by a lone pilot in a small rec-flier. Each was asked to trade scanning equipment. None admitted to any dealings with the pilot.

Those who bothered to record details of the encounters confirm the identity as the Turcanian of GB5478.

I have no documentary evidence to send you, as none of the captains was willing to be identified.

I hope this is of some use to you in your data gathering.

Yours warmly,
MS

[Received January 20, 2199 O4#JD-6200]

From: AA.rc.mna

To: OFFICE of External Affairs, Earth, Sol

MY friend and esteemed benefactor, colleague and brother to my father's ambitions, the Captain James Bartholomew, of the Jovian Corporative Organization.
HE passed to me certain informations, that you need of reports in the following paths.
MY ship, a trader of great worth.
WE find ourselves in work at Orion-the First by the second moon.
HERE, at the end of our work, we have hails.
NEAR us in the orbit above, this is the craft of one person.
HE with large eyes and a manner not of a trader.
TURCANIA his home.
TURCANIS Major- the Fifth, I think to you.
ALAS, not always my father's son, I make no profit with this person.
THE trade he wish to make.
THINGS of many questionable note, and of such quantities as I much wonder.
I wish no part, for the sake of my customers, my crew, and my father's honor.
NO trade I make with this person, though he with much persistence argue and shout.
THE craft he flies.
THIS we know.
PRAESTANS Rapax, near to Oraga – the Beta.
HERE they make most cunning and craft of much worth.
TURCANIAN is a person of great riches, in flying thus.
THIS is my information.
NEAR your path I hope it lies.
WITH this then I greet you, of the Office of External Affairs.
ALL that is good and wondrous in our skies.
THIS to be yours in your goings.

AA.rc.mna

Give me strength - how do these guys ever do business with each other? What's the point of having Standard?

a)   If the Turcanian's ship is that small where is he going to put these 'quantities'?
b)   I hear the Turcanian is peaceful and if anything a little dim, no one else has even whispered he has a bad temper.

File this under 'Doubtful'.

Liz
January 24 2199

[Received February 4, 2199 O1#A1-5231]
[Prioritized 01#EC-4300]

From: Patrol Commandant Ngell Amarno, Hawkins Array, Horsehead Nebula

To: Elizabeth Curacao, OEA, Dept. EA

February 4, 2199

GB5478 – Confirmed sighting of Turcanian

I wish to inform you that as a consequence of an arrest made at the culmination of a criminal investigation into the activities outlined below, we have come into possession of information regarding an inhabitant of the Turcanis Major system.

Local trader, Melha Melha, has been found guilty of selling prohibited technology in three counts.

Count One:
On November 12, 2198, sold five (5) high yield oxygen grenades to a junior Astran diplomat
Count Two:
On November 15, 2198, sold ten crates of compressed gas rifles to an Ursalan political group
Count Three:
On November 19, 2198, sold one medical laser scalpel, with instruction manual, to a minor

Further information: please reference 154673/HA/NA/9987

During the surveillance of Count Three, my officers recorded the sale of

One Ultra-High-Definition Infra-Red Detector
Containing:
    One UHD IRD Base, Control and Actuation Unit
    Twenty-five distributed scanning nodes, remote transceivers and central base converter
    One set Documentation
    Two maintenance kits

The purchaser was identified as the individual described in GB5478.
He identified himself as Edward from Turcania.
He paid in platinum strips.
No prohibition exists against trade with Turcanis Major. No charges have been brought with regard to this sale.

Please contact this station if further information is required.

P.Comm. Amarno

Memo from Office of External Affairs

From: Elizabeth Curacao, OEA, Dept. EA

To: Section Chief Tomkins, EIA

February 15, 2199

Re: First Contact/Techno Trading

Attached is an informational from the HH Neb, with ref to Turcanis Major.

Surveys had identified one sentient race in this system. No contact has been made, with the exception of this one trader.

Should we be worried about the nature of this contact?

Liz

Memo from External Intelligence Agency

From: Lucy Fry, Analyst, EIA

To: E. Curucao, OEA

February 20, 2199

Ms. Curucao,

Thank you for your recent memo to Mr. Tomkins in reference to techno-trades with Torcanis Major.

We know of no regulations against trade with this system.

Thank you for your correspondence.

Lucy Fry.

Memo from Office of External Affairs

From: Elizabeth Curacao, OEA, Dept. EA

To: Section Chief Tomkins, EIA

February 20, 2199

Re: Turcanis Major

Please confirm by reply to this memo, that it is your professional judgment that high-tech trades to this unknown race pose no actual or potential threat to Earth, its interests, or those of its allies.

Thank you for your individual attention.

Elizabeth Curacao

Memo from External Intelligence Agency

From: Lucy Fry, Analyst, EIA

To: E. Curacao, OEA

February 22, 2199

Ms. Curacao,

Thank you for your recent memo to Mr. Tomkins in reference to techno-trades with Turcanis Major.

Mr. Tomkins asks that you send the entire file on this matter for his review. Thank you for your prompt attention.

Lucy Fry

Memo from External Intelligence Agency

From: Section Chief Tomkins

To: Liz Curacao, OEA

February 25, 2199

Liz,

The information you sent is not sufficient for us to develop an opinion on Turcanis Major.

I confess that it is an unusual way for a race to announce itself to the galaxy, but it would be paranoia to assume malign intent.

I shall authorize covert surveillance of Turcanis Major for a period of three months.

Please refer future correspondence on this matter to Analyst Lucy Fry.

Tomkins

Extracts from
Surveillance Analysis of Turcanis Major V-I performed from March 15, 2199 to June 15, 2199 by Lucy Fry

The people of TMV-I show no interest in the rest of the galaxy. Their transmissions are mainly from a single entertainment organization....

...There are signs of increasing use of encrypted computer transactions. These are believed to be of a business-related nature....

...Since the original survey of the system we see an increase in technological sophistication, but no more interest in astronomy. They have no astronomical satellites. They have several communication relays, but no orbital stations. They send up machines, but not people....

...We see in their entertainment clear images of their people. The figure in the First Contact reports matches closely the anatomy and bearing of these people. However, in light of their state of interest in space travel, this may be a coincidence....

...We see in their transmissions a population that is varied in culture and belief. There are several different religions. People in different geographical regions dress differently. There seems to be one common language, with regional variations....

Great. "People in different geographical regions dress differently." Who is this idiot?

I'm becoming more and more concerned about our future in the EIA's hands.

Liz
August 4, 2199

Internal Memo
Office of External Affairs

From: Elizabeth Curacao

To: Michaelo Korvanotualli

August 5, 2199

Mike,

I still have a bad feeling about the Turcanian trader.

Tomkins says I'm paranoid. But I have zero confidence in the EIA analysis.

We still have no idea why he wanted such a high-end IR scanner. We can hope it's for a peaceful use but we are completely in the dark.

I think, since they have voluntarily broken their isolation by trading, we should initiate a second contact.

Perhaps through their government(s) we can get to meet this 'Edward' character and finally get to the bottom of this.

We also have competing FC01s. We have to sort out who gets the fee before we get a reputation for non-payment.

What do you think?

Liz.

Liz, from what I see this is an underdeveloped small population.
I don't think the potential warrants a full scale diplo mission. We can't detract from our other efforts.
Is there anyone we can send who isn't busy right now- semi-officially?
I'm ok with you doing enough to satisfy your curiosity, but nothing major. Ok?

Mike K.

LIZ – meeting

TURCANIS MAJOR V – 1

trader – 'Edward'

IR HIGH-DEF ?

No space travel

2nd Contact   Gov – then trader ←

DON'T START A WAR!

EIA – Lucy Fry – language tuition

JIM ABLE OFFWORLD

SOPHA

2

ED CHARLTON

AUTHOR OF "THE ALERONDE TRILOGY"

CHAPTER FIVE

The moment the green dawn lit Sopha's face, the Regdenir spoke a single word, the others began to sing, and to Jim's lasting astonishment, Turcanis Major V burst over the horizon.

Nothing had prepared Jim for what he saw. Mainworld seemed pleasant enough when he had held station above it. It had oceans and continents, clouds and storms, much like any other planet. Now, refracted through the atmosphere of its largest moon, it looked far different. The green glow was more than the reflected sunlight. This was like the sun shining through the leaf of a living plant. It gave him a thrill of wonder as the world changed color around him. He felt as awed as at the approach of a majestic animal. Jim felt as if he were watching Life itself appear before him.

As the planet cleared the horizon, its hold over him lessened. The green fire faded, and familiar details returned somewhat. It seemed to shrink a little, becoming more like a massive jewel, precious and fascinating. Jim looked over to the Regdenir, taken up in their worship; he looked back to the planet and understood. Not moving or thinking, he allowed himself to be absorbed in the sight.

Sopha was at Jim's side, looking earnestly into his face.

"It's beautiful," Jim said softly.

"It is Beauty."

They continued to watch the risen planet for a few more minutes before Sopha motioned for Jim to follow. They walked to the very edge of the platform and gazed together at the long drop below. A river ran down either side of the landing strip. Jim could see the water surging up, through, and around the elaborate roots of trees at the valley's edge.

Sopha began to speak in Standard once more. "You are fortunate to come when Beauty is full, and her path is at night. This is a festival time in the cities. Every eye is on Beauty tonight. You see why I urged you to arrive in daylight? Every Regdenir alive would have seen your craft."

Jim nodded and looked again at the planet dominating the sky. He laughed, a broad smile relaxing his face. For the first time in many long months, his spirit was soaring.

"Our ancestors," began Sopha, "were mathematicians and astronomers. The root of our religion is in mathematics. I dare say the audnir do not mention that. These mathematicians knew how to measure distance using shadows and angles. Do you have a word in Standard for this?"

"Trigonometry."

"Hmm, yes. This is the science they knew. Our first Holy Works are the B'Metir, a set of drawings showing the distance between Beauty and us, between us and the sun. Then come the paths of our worlds as they orbit the sun. Those great minds knew the sizes of each dancer in this play."

"What of other worlds and the galaxy?"

Sopha nodded. "Yes, they deduced that other suns would have other planets. They knew about all these things. Against the scale of the galaxy, *this*—that you see rising before you—is as nothing, merely a one-dimensional point, occupying no discernible place in the great scheme of things. That they could calculate this from their observations alone humbles us today."

He began to walk Jim around the edge of the platform farther from the tunnel's mouth and the valley wall. The rock was a delicate pale green in the planet light, its patterns and drawings starkly black.

"Yet they knew what you now know. It is *beautiful*. How can it be that something so insignificant can be so beautiful? It was a puzzle that was long in the solving—more so than the mere numerical calculations. It was a puzzle of the spirit as much as of the mind. The key to our belief, James Able, is in the 'nearly' and the 'almost.' Beauty is *almost* nothing, *nearly* a mathematical point. But it does have mass; it does occupy a physical space. It has a diameter. It has weight. It has motion and gravity. That is the dividing line. That is the nexus. However small it may be, it does exist, and it is beautiful. Thus the universe is changed."

He was silent, seemingly having said all he needed. Jim was about to begin asking questions when the Regdenir spoke again.

"The universe is a cold and empty place, James Able. There is no comfort for flesh and blood in the vacuum. In the scorching hearts of stars or the dead rocks of old worlds, there is nothing for us. We look at them and quake in our hearts. For all our thoughts and feelings, space is far deeper than we can hope to conceive, far longer than we can hope to tell, far taller than all our highest ambitions combined. Perhaps, then, we should all despair and quail at the vastness and be overwhelmed at the impersonal coldness of it all?" He paused, apparently expecting no answer. "But no. We know something else about the universe. We, here on this rock, know something that no one else knows. We know that Beauty exists. Against all the terrors that have been created amongst the stars stands this. This, too, was made. This, too, has its place in the galaxy. The picture is not complete without this. With Beauty in that picture, therefore, it is not all horror and despair. Knowing that Beauty has a place is what changes everything."

They continued their walk along the rim of the platform until they were at its western end. With the planet suspended above them, the arching lines and inscriptions stood out clearly in their intricacy and complexity.

"It is like this, James Able. Beauty is a flame, lit in a dark room.

No matter how small the flame, the darkness of the room is held back all the while the flame burns. Also, Beauty is like a face. It is the face of a lover, one face shining amongst a vast crowd of strangers."

He turned to face Jim and, clasping him by the shoulders, spoke in an authoritative voice that split the quiet of the night and sent the electricity of surprise through Jim's limbs.

"You asked me a question! Why do we refer to our planet as Beauty? *Look!* Ask yourself! *Look!*"

He stepped to Jim's side but held onto his shoulders, one arm pressing across Jim's chest. Jim was staring straight at the planet, its soft light transfixing him.

Sopha's voice was urgent, whispering in his ear, "The universe is made beautiful, whatever else it holds, because it also holds this!" He paused.

Jim was aware of Sopha's breath on the side of his face, and his legs tingled in the awareness of the long drop behind his heels.

"Because of this fact, James Able, we know there is also a place for love and hope and truth." He released his formidable grip on Jim's shoulders and resumed his usual tone. "This is our belief. This is our task. We stand before the universe, holding up the one small candle."

Jim looked again into the face of Beauty. So this was their answer to Einstein's question: Is the universe friendly?

No, but...

Jim and Sopha were alone on the promontory. Jim had neither seen nor heard the others leave.

The path back in only planet-light was slow and difficult. Jim suspected that Turcanian eyes were better adapted to low light than his. When they came out of the ferns behind the house, its windows already shone with light, and the smells of food were in the air.

Although Sopha's sons served and did not speak, two other Regdenir were at the meal and answered if addressed. Their use of modern Turcanian was interspersed with archaic references that slowed conversation somewhat. Jim wondered if they might consider his attendance at the ceremony somewhat heretical. They did not say so in his hearing.

Sopha spent some time decrying the audnir for never looking up at Beauty, for locking themselves in their houses at night.

"Even though they have 'rediscovered' astronomy, they are blind to what they are seeing."

Finally, Jim had the opportunity to ask his questions. "Why do you need to own an infrared scanner?" he asked with an involuntary sigh.

Sopha laughed. "You are of a single mind, James Able. There is a fish in the seas to the south of Appinar that, when it bites, will never let go. You truly have found your calling in life, have you not?"

Jim frowned. "As we discussed earlier, I have great doubts about that."

Sopha shook his head. "No, doubt yourself no more. All who breathe make mistakes. We all make the wrong choice at some time. We learn best when we err most."

One of Sopha's sons placed a dish of long purple stems on the table in front of his father. Sopha took a cup of orange powder and sprinkled it over the stems. To Jim's disgust, the stems began to writhe and twitch.

"Can you ingest food with sulfuric acid?"

"It depends on the concentration, I think," Jim answered, hoping for a way out of eating it.

Sopha nodded. "Then do not take the behrra. The longer they take to die, the stronger the acid. Within a few minutes, if you drop one on the table, it will burn the wood."

"Are they animals?"

"They are a primitive form of life. We see them fossilized in many places."

Jim watched as they all ate with obvious relish. He said, "May I ask an easier question?"

Sopha said, "Begin."

"We received news of you from a shopkeeper on a station at Arietis. We also heard from the captain of a trade ship owned by Himdu-Cola. Do you remember which of them you talked with first?"

Sopha stopped chewing for a moment and smiled. "No."

Jim shrugged. "Oh well." He guessed Liz wasn't going to like that answer. "And can you confirm for me again that neither of them made any arrangements with you to meet people from Earth?"

Sopha's eyes flashed. He said, "I had no such desire! I met many people. You know this already! I had no desire for any more contact."

Jim waited a moment and then said with a smile, "So what is it about the scanner? Why was it so important to you to own one?"

Sopha did not smile back. He looked into the distance with a solemn expression.

"Did Madhar Nect tell you of the audnir's greatest sin?"

"I... I don't think so."

"Eighty-nine years ago, they defiled Beauty."

"Ah...the spaceship."

Sopha nodded. "They sent a foul machine to touch the face of Beauty. They dared to go there and walk upon it as if it were no more than the dirt of the street."

Jim said nothing, waiting to hear more. Sopha pushed away his plate, a behrra still squirming in its death throes.

"Not only did they defile it, but the machinery they used to land will have *burnt* the Holy Ground. And now to the answer of your most persistent question." Sopha's eyes flashed under his brows. "The craft they used left behind a...relaunch module. There remain discarded parts, burnt and leaking foul chemicals into the atmosphere of Beauty."

Jim frowned and asked, "And you want to pinpoint where they are?"

"I will find them. I will go there. I will remove them."

"Oh, I see."

"The main task I set myself was the procurement of a spaceworthy craft. It had to be one that would cause minimum damage on takeoff and would leave no foul discharges in its wake as it traveled. This I found with comparative ease and had delivered to this place by a most discreet supplier. A person, I may say, who did not ask questions as you do. The scanner was a secondary thought and proved much more troublesome to find."

Jim nodded and smiled at his host. "I see. I understand. Thank you. Thank you, Sopha Luca, on behalf of the Office of External Affairs."

Sopha bowed his head but flashed his eyes again at Jim.

"And, now, let me ask you perhaps a personal question?"

"Okay."

"In the picture I found of you, your face was different. We spoke earlier of details. I am curious that people from Earth change their appearance."

Jim was taken aback. He could not think of any way his appearance was different, except his clothing.

"I...I am not sure I know what you mean."

Sopha reached out, and his rough finger touched Jim's right cheek, beside his nose, and again along his jawline.

"Here and here. You are different."

"Ah...yes...yes. You're right! When I was injured—at Ch'Garratt —I was burned down this side of my face. The picture showed some scar tissue that had built up in the healing process. I had it removed quite recently."

"How is this done?"

"Oh, a laser scalpel. It's very simple. They just burn the dead tissue off."

Sopha did not understand. "Please explain."

"Are you familiar with lasers? Stimulated light. If you focus particular frequencies of light in the right way, it can burn through things. There are many examples of them in civilian and military use."

Sopha shook his head. "No, you are mistaken. I remember now. I have seen this device. It is a child's toy!"

"No, it's not at all a toy."

"Yes...yes. I have seen one...a laser scalpel...that was its name. Where I purchased the scanner, the trader sold one to a small boy. It is a toy, James Able, a toy!"

Jim had to think back to the original briefing file. The trader had been arrested; that was how Sopha was spotted. Yes, he was arrested for selling something to a minor. Was it a scalpel?

"Okay...I think I know what happened. The trader you dealt with...did not...was not always trading within the law. What he sold was not a toy and should never have been given to a minor."

"Such things are dangerous, then?"

"Sure. You can do a lot of damage with any laser. Think about it. It's a beam of light that can go enormous distances at about— what is it for you?—400 million murtel per second and, with the right configuration, vaporize whatever it hits! It's no toy. It's a serious offense to sell them where they might be misused."

Sopha was silent, staring into the distance again. He turned his face toward Jim but said nothing. Jim wondered if he had offended the Turcanian in some way. But then Sopha smiled and called over one of his sons.

"Bring the Redille. It is a special occasion. Tonight we celebrate the questions of James Able."

"And the answers of Sopha Luca," Jim added politely.

Redille was a viscous alcoholic beverage. Happily, Sopha only poured one measure for each of them and then had the bottle put away. After they had drunk, Sopha seemed more excited and animated than Jim had yet seen him. The conversation strayed back to the audnir spacecraft.

"You understand, James Able, that the defilement on Beauty must be removed?"

"I understand. It is sad that they used such limited technology. Using a craft like yours would not leave any pollution."

"No! Have you not listened to anything I have taught you? They must not go back in *any* craft!"

Oops, Jim thought to himself.

Sopha continued, "The audnir defiled Beauty with their presence once. It cannot be permitted again. I cannot go back in time and undo the defilement, but I can remove some of its consequences."

"Are you sure it's okay for *you* to go?"

Sopha hesitated. "It has been a topic of discussion for nearly ninety years. Many great thinkers have written about it. I shall be bringing the matter to some closure."

Jim understood more than Sopha had perhaps intended to say. "You're putting yourself at risk."

"Even by traveling away from home, I may have offended many. Yes, you are right; there will be those who think I go too far. I even run the risk of having all my contributions wrapped around with secure commentaries within the Regdekol, to be visible only to my superiors. The stakes are high, James Able. I appreciated your comment, from before we met, that I do not act 'on a whim.' The stakes are high."

Jim got up from the table and walked to the window. The dining room, like the fountain room, looked out onto the landing strip and his flier.

"What a day!" he said aloud.

Sopha was watching him from the table. "Are you thinking of your journey back?"

"Yes. I should be going soon."

"Then there is but one piece of business left to us."

"What's that?" said Jim, turning.

"The recording. Now you know why I cannot let you encourage the audnir to think of space travel. It is better that you do not appear to them. Knowledge of other races and other worlds, as you yourself wrote, will mean they will try again to explore this system. Then they will defile Beauty in their ignorance. I told you we stand against the darkness in the universe. The audnir know only darkness and spread it wherever they go. They are lost to us, but we have a responsibility not to let them loose on the galaxy. We can never let them loose on Beauty."

At that moment, Jim hoped, more than any other time in his life, the ground would open and swallow him. "I..."

"The recording, James Able. I must now have the recording."

The silence in the room was cold and sad.

"I don't have it. I doubt I can get it," he said quietly.

"You wrote that you had secured it!"

"I could arrange only a postponement of the transmission. I needed the time...to work out how to appease both you and Madhar Nect."

"Do you realize what you have done?"

Sopha's whole head was flushed. His eyes flashed across the room. His sons were looking at Jim, aware that something had suddenly made their father angry.

"Agh! You are audnir! I knew I should not trust you. You will contact Nect *now*! You will keep your bargain with me!"

His voice seemed to fill not only the room but the whole valley at Jim's back. He led Jim into the computer room and activated one of the monitors along a side wall. He pointed at the chair, and Jim lowered himself into it.

"You will instruct the audnir Nect what she is to do. You will remain with us until this matter is satisfactorily resolved."

Sopha turned away from Jim and barked instructions to his sons. One of them said something in surprise. Sopha swiped his fist across the boy's face, knocking him back into the doorframe. Sopha grabbed his arm and pushed him out of the room, shouting all the while. Jim understood none of the words but all of the emotion. He took several deep breaths.

▭

madhar∇nect∇latsin∇ux

Greetings, my fellow scientist and helper, Madhar Nect.

I have spent time with Sopha Luca and now understand much more of what you told me.

Perhaps I was hasty in granting you permission to record our discussion. Perhaps my presence will inspire a new space program. Perhaps the Regdenir have reasons for wishing you not to explore this system. Perhaps my presence will stir bad feelings again between yourselves and the Regdenir.

Then Sopha Luca is right to keep me here. Then it is appropriate that you bring all copies of the recording to this place. Then I trust you will once more help me in my task, for which I thank you.

Your friend, James Able.

aaaaVjiirVregde99Vapp

CHAPTER SIX

"I don't know how quickly she will reply. Won't she be asleep now?" Jim asked.

"It doesn't matter, as long as she does what you ask. I wonder that here might not be the best place for her to come. I do not want her to know this place. Perhaps we can find another..."

Jim shrugged. "How will she come? She doesn't have a flier, like mine or yours."

"The audnir have aircraft, but they will not be able to land anywhere in the forest but here."

Sopha held his hand to his head and gave a shrill squeak. Jim wondered if this was a noise of pain or of panic.

"You will send her the location information. I will need to move after she has gone. This is not good, James Able. This will cost me much, both in time and resources."

"I'm sorry. I truly am."

"You are audnir. Your sorrow is nothing to me."

While Jim sent the second message, Sopha stepped away and called out to his sons. One of them came running in from outside. Jim overheard the instruction to have Sopha's flier ready to launch at a moment's notice.

Jim's mind was already working in overdrive. Sopha was still paranoid about secrecy and was strategizing about trouble from Madhar Nect. That meant Jim had to be looking for a chance to take advantage of anything that happened. All he had to do was keep his head down until the scientist arrived. If the worst came to the worst, Nect would lose her interview. Jim didn't think that was too big a problem.

After a few minutes of waiting and not receiving a reply from Madhar Nect, Sopha led Jim back to the fountain room. Here two of his sons were waiting. They carried what were unmistakably weapons, and they were pointed at him.

"Go with them" was all Sopha said.

The room they locked him in was small and bare. Beauty shone through a skylight above him. Jim sat on the low bed and sighed.

I've done it again, haven't I? Ch'Garratt could look like a picnic compared with how bad this could get. What if Nect comes with troops, and they blast their way through the Regdenir?

These and other dark thoughts swirled through Jim's head as he waited. He stretched out on the bed and looked up at the face of the planet.

Standing on the promontory staring up into the night, Sopha had so inspired him; his thoughts had seemed to broaden. Yet his stomach churned at the memory of Sopha's violence toward his son.

As he gazed at Mainworld, his focus drifted back to the window itself and to its frame. The pale green light was reflecting off the hinges and the catch. "You idiot!" he said quietly to himself.

He could not reach the catch. Even standing on the bed, it was beyond his grasp. He quietly tipped the bed onto its side. Jamming one end up against the door secured it enough for Jim to balance on the board that ran along the bed's side. With some effort, he forced the skylight open and hauled himself out onto the roof.

Lying flat on his stomach, he moved to peer over the north side of the roof. He could see the pale swath of the landing strip, Beauty reflecting off the dull metal of his flier. Jim's heart lifted. Perhaps he could just climb aboard and be gone from this difficult little moon. As he watched, a cloaked figure walked out from behind the flier, the blue cloak black in the soft light. Jim could not see the gun, but something in the angle of the arm told him it was there. Easy flight was not an option. Even as that hope died, he realized why he couldn't just run: he had to be there when Nect arrived. He would have to try to fix the mess he had made. The best he could do for now was to ensure that Sopha didn't have him at gunpoint.

He slid around to look toward the other building; a light was showing from inside. The sounds, carried on the warm air, were of someone preparing Sopha's flier.

Jim lay still and formulated half a plan. Maybe he would try to get inside Sopha's flier. When they noticed he was gone, they might not search there. Also, if things got ugly when Nect showed up, the flier itself could be useful.

He heard a knock on the door of his room below, then Sopha's voice saying something. Scrambling back to the skylight, he lowered his shoulders back into the room.

"What did you say?" he called out.

Sopha answered, "Nect has replied. She says she understands the situation and will come after daybreak. I hope we can yet resolve this, James Able."

"Sure," said Jim, still hanging into the room. He heard Sopha walk back into the main part of the house.

He lay on the roof for a while, staring up at Beauty and the stars. He was relying on Madhar Nect to understand the situation more clearly than Sopha. Nect had hopefully read the word "hostage" between Jim's carefully chosen phrases. As he lay there, he could hear Sopha talking to one of his sons. It sounded like he was over by the flier's shed. Jim rolled over to watch. He saw them both return to the main house.

I wonder..., he thought.

He crawled over to the back end of the house and looked down. It was a short drop, but in the half-light, he could not be sure what he would land on. He moved around the edge of the roof on all fours. At the point nearest the shed, the light shone enough for him to see clearly the ground beneath. Unfortunately, he would also be in clear view of the guard over by his own flier.

He waited an hour or more.

Surely even Regdenir have to relieve themselves sometime?

He watched the young Turcanian start to come back to the house several times and resist before his discomfort finally overcame his orders. As soon as he dashed into the house, Jim lowered himself over the edge and down onto the ground. He ran, half-crouched, over to the shadow of the shed. He waited there, listening. There were no sounds of movement from within.

Sopha's flier was a dream machine. The Praestans Rapax Company was the best. They catered to the richest, or fussiest, of the galaxy's travelers. This was a model Jim had not seen before. It was sleek, almost to the point of being a stealth flier. Its black enamel body was an elegant V-wing: the cockpit slightly recessed, the sensor modules slightly extended.

Jim cautiously stepped up the ramp and found himself in a leather and wood navigation suite. The cockpit opened to one side, the kitchen to the other. He shook his head at the contrast to his rental. He walked through the kitchen to the small but stylish sleeping area. He would wait there, he decided, until Nect, and whatever help she brought with her, arrived. If anyone came searching, he could hide in the decon unit.

He sat on the bed, in the dark, and waited. He would have done things differently had he known. He had believed Nect's dismissal of the Regdenir. That had been his mistake. He should have remembered that, in every dispute, there are two sides, and to judge after hearing only one side was foolish. Perhaps Nect did not know how the Regdenir viewed themselves. Jim couldn't help thinking that Sopha's view of his own responsibility—to his work, to Beauty, to the universe—was in a weird way inspiring.

Jim knew he didn't have that attitude. He prided himself on his practicality, on being able to do enough to get by, but it seemed dull and lifeless compared with Sopha's passion. He remembered how his face had looked, reflected in the water of the fountain. He felt more pale and ragged now than he had then.

And then, after all the danger, the potential trouble ahead, the possibility of friendship with the Regdenir dashed by the way he'd handled things, Jim finally knew one thing for certain: Sopha Luca couldn't remember which first contact claimant he had spoken to first. The mission had failed. He wouldn't be able to justify a payment to either of them. Unresolved claims meant tedious paperwork going back and forth for years to come.

Just before dawn, the Regdenir discovered Jim's absence. As the voices of the forest began to return, they were mixed with shouts from Sopha. Just as the first beams of sunlight hit the mountain peaks, the forest sounds changed. A deep throb of flying machinery was echoing down the valley. Madhar Nect and friends were moving in, keeping the sun behind them.

Sopha was not there to greet them. Six Turcanian military helicopters landed on the strip. The two Regdenir, who had eaten with Jim the previous evening, stood unmoving in front of Jim's flier. They waited until the rotor blades had stilled and thirty heavily armed soldiers had massed between their craft.

"Why have you broken the Agreement of Rubaw? Why have you brought weapons into the land reserved for the Regdenir?" called one of them.

Madhar Nect and a senior commander walked through the ranks and stood face to face with them. The commander spoke. "Where is Sopha Luca, and where is the alien? Answer immediately or be arrested for conspiracy."

"Neither Sopha Luca nor his family is accepting visitors. Nor will he accept visitors who arrive bearing weapons."

"Listen, you people," interrupted Madhar Nect, sighing, "this is going to get ugly if we don't cooperate. *You* want us to go without a fuss. *You* don't want this to become a major incident. *We* want to go without a fuss. *We* don't want a major incident." She continued, "It's very simple. We give you a recording. We take the alien. No problem. Okay?"

"The alien is missing," said one of the Regdenir quietly.

Madhar turned and spat on the ground. "Great."

. . .

Jim had heard the arrival of the helicopters. That no shots had been fired encouraged him greatly. He decided to see what was happening.

Sopha was standing facing him as he walked into the flier's kitchen.

"James Able."

"Sopha Luca. Good morning."

"No, James Able, this is the blackest morning we have seen in four hundred years. Since our ancestors were driven out to the marshes, no troops have come into our land. You have brought this upon us. I should kill you where you stand. You have lied, tricked, and cheated your way into my house and into our most holy worship, and now look what you have done."

Jim was going to apologize, but Sopha continued.

"I will not let you, or any other, stand in the way of my work. I have chosen a path; I must follow it, whatever the cost. It no longer matters about the audnir. Go with them, quickly, before I break your back and throw you to them!"

He stood back to let Jim pass. With a deep breath Jim stepped forward. Sopha bared his teeth and hissed at him as he rushed through the navigation room and out of the flier. His appearance at the door of the shed was greeted by a buzz from the troops and Madhar Nect.

"Jim Able! Are you hurt?" called the scientist.

"No, I'm fine."

He ran toward them, smiling. He saw the surprise on the faces of the two Regdenir. The commander and Madhar Nect moved to meet Jim near the other end of his flier.

"I am Rulpha Quar. You are Jim Able of Earth?"

"I am. Thank you for coming. I am sorry to have caused this problem."

"We will escort you to a safe place. I see you have your own transport."

Jim thought he detected a smirk on the officer's face, but he wasn't sure.

The roof of the building behind him exploded. Sopha's flier

scattered glass and wood toward them as it lunged into the air. Everyone ducked to the ground except Jim, who stood open-mouthed, staring at the flier as it shuddered, almost failing to reach sufficient momentum to continue its ascent.

He knew what was going to happen. The flier would turn. It would open fire. This time he would not survive.

Sopha wrestled his struggling flier until it groaned with the structural stress. Then he lifted the nose and once more left the atmosphere of his home moon.

Jim sank to his knees and vomited, much to the disgust of the Turcanians picking themselves off the ground around him.

Jim was escorted to a Turcanian city on the border of the Regdenir area. Its military base was on high alert, and he was directed to park his flier in a huge hanger that had been emptied for the occasion.

Madhar Nect accompanied him to his first official briefing.

"Relax. They'll just want to be sure you're not going to invade. Really, that's their only worry. They know they can't defend us against your technology. It scares the crap out of them, knowing there's nothing they can do about it."

"I'm sure they could defend themselves against me."

"What about the fleet of warships clustered around our brother moon?"

Jim smiled. "Oh, don't worry about them. It's only my fan club."

"That's what I mean. Don't joke with them. They're military; they've had their humor surgically removed."

Jim nodded, acknowledging Madhar's serious expression. "Understood."

He worked the meeting from the script he had been trained to use for second contact situations. The protocols were simple; so was his message. He gave gifts of Standard language training modules to anyone who wanted one. He gave sheets of written instructions on how to duplicate the training devices and the language data. He gave information on which radio frequencies to use and which to avoid using. He said nothing about Sopha other than he had met him.

He welcomed Turcanis Major V-I to the rest of the galaxy.

The military questioners asked about his weaponry. He almost got a smile out of them as he described his experience renting the flier. He began to guess that some of these officers had had some low-gravity training in aircraft. From that, he learned that the space program was more than just a distant memory. Thanks to Madhar's prompting, he was able to excite his questioners with talk of trade in advanced technology. He did not mention the restrictions and galactic laws that governed all such matters. They would find out soon enough when the matter was safely in the hands of the civilian government.

In a comfortable room after the briefing, Jim sat chatting with Madhar. "I really wanted to avoid being the cause of unpleasantness between you and the Regdenir. Can you arrange to have that side of things...de-emphasized?"

The scientist frowned. "Why? What does it matter?"

Jim sighed. "I guess it's a personal thing. I get the impression that they're, with one exception, really okay. They have their reasons for things, you know. They're not as...," he smiled, "daft as you might think."

Madhar shook her head. "Don't think you can come and solve one of our longest and most intractable sociological problems after a couple of days hanging around in orbit. It's not that easy."

"I know. I just...I don't want to be the cause of any trouble."

"Look, it's not your fault. You didn't start anything. The Regdenir are, and always have been, aggressive, insular, and irrational. The only way they will deal with other people is on their own terms. Everyone has to bend to their way of doing things and their thinking. There has never been any compromise with them. So we deal with it as best we can. I'm still embarrassed—shocked, even—that our first contact with the wider galaxy was through *them*. It's inconceivable."

"It can cause problems when a planet hasn't gotten its act together, you know. There are too many races around out there to keep track of the factions within each one. You're all one to us. Put on a blue cloak, and to the rest of the galaxy, there's no difference."

Madhar shook her head again. "That's going to be the toughest thing we ever do. That mind-set is as alien as that bubble you call a head."

They were silent for a while.

"He wants to remove the trash left over from the spacecraft you put on Mainworld."

"What?"

"That's what this has all been about. He's going there to clean up after you guys."

Madhar laughed and nodded her head. "What did I tell you? What did I tell you?"

They smiled at each other and were quiet again. The scientist looked into the distance and buzzed.

"I wonder what the Maggnir will make of another visit?"

Jim felt something burst in his head.

"Who?"

"The Maggnir."

"You told me 'Magg' was the old name for Mainworld. You didn't tell me there was a 'nir' there."

"Didn't I? Sure there are people there. Our astronauts saw evidence of them during their explorations. They're really way behind us. The thinking at the time was they would be calling on us in about two to three thousand years' time."

Jim shook his head hard, but it didn't help. How could his information have been so wrong?

"They have agriculture. They have some metalwork, so they're on the right track. We don't know how many of them there are, of course, because we've never been back. Maybe they'll surprise us and be calling before we think."

"That's the kind of first contact I would love to witness."

"Not in our lifetimes, Jim Able. We have to leave some of the fun for our descendants. Now, you promised me another interview..."

· · ·

Jim was relieved to see how much at ease all the Turcanians were with him. The TV production crew treated him with the same disrespect they showered on Madhar. There were many jokes about his makeup, about not knowing how much was too much, or that people would think the whole head was an artificial creation. There was even a practical joke played on him: he was presented with a gift that contained some kind of furry animal, which came bursting out of the wrapping as he began to open it. Madhar had to explain that it was a fashion among Turcanian children at birthday celebrations—the fun being not knowing which parcel might be alive.

They had decided not to show any of Madhar and Jim's first conversation. The light was not good; the sound was too low. In true infotainment style, the crew of *Madhar Nect's Science World* recreated the whole thing, properly lit, properly recorded. Jim had to land his flier in Madhar's field eight times before they were happy.

Near the end of the filming, Jim was introduced to three visiting dignitaries from the ruling alliance. They seemed, to Jim, to be wary of him. One, in particular, avoided his eyes and spoke seldom.

Coordinator Huratt said to Jim, "You know your arrival is a little ill-timed?"

"Why is that?"

"We have elections for our municipalities in two weeks. This is all...rather distracting."

"I'm sorry; I don't see..."

"Our majority is thin. Well, anyone's majority is thin in our system. But this year especially, we need our voters to be focused, you understand?"

Jim frowned and shook his head.

"Well, I don't want to seem ungrateful that you've come all this way. It's just that it is rather ill-timed. I'm sure you'll understand."

With that, they shook his hand and shuffled off, leaving Jim none the wiser. Later, when he had a moment with Madhar, he asked her about it.

"What did they say to you?"

"I...nothing. They didn't say anything. Huratt talked about my visit being 'ill-timed' and their majority being 'thin.' That was it!"

"Ah," said the scientist knowingly.

"'Ah' what?"

Madhar nodded and said, "Yes. You are the biggest distraction we've ever had around an election."

"So?"

"Remember, I told you our politics are fluid. Our alliances rarely last long. Your presence will tip the elections in favor of the parties that support outward-looking policies, the science funding—what some refer to as the 'liberal agenda.'"

"Why?"

"The conservative elements in our society are based in a history similar to the insularity of the Regdenir. They don't see the need to look up or out or across to each other. They believe in people looking after themselves. You are forcing voters to consider wider issues."

Jim shook his head. "I feared yesterday that I was going to be the cause of a war between you and the Regdenir; now you're telling me I'm going to decide an election! I'm in so much trouble back home."

"Why?"

"I was supposed to find out who Sopha was, who he first made contact with, and to say to your government 'Hello, we're out here.' Nothing more. I wasn't supposed to change anything!"

Madhar stared at Jim in disbelief.

"Jim, listen to me. Nothing can possibly be a greater change than to hear that we're not alone! We've all grown up, as did our ancestors, aware of the tantalizing possibility that there was other life out there in space but never knowing for sure. When we found the Maggnir, it was a shock, but it could be explained away and still leave this the only habitable system in the galaxy. But now we know! This is a major, major change for us. How could you think it would be otherwise? Listen, you could go up and paint Mainworld purple, and it would have less of an impact on us than this TV show is going to have!"

Jim weighed their situation. "If you'd known what Sopha Luca was up to—if you'd known what he knew—then I wouldn't be news, would I?"

"Yes, you would, being the first. But the change would have already happened. You're right, there."

"We assumed this was a second contact. It's not—it's a first. You see, I shouldn't be doing this."

CHAPTER SEVEN

Jim stayed in orbit to watch the show. It was a slick production. Madhar came out looking earnest and sober. Jim felt that the visiting alien looked like a grinning idiot with too much makeup.

During the after-broadcast party, Jim contacted Madhar through the voice unit.

"How do you think it went, my friend?" she asked him.

"I looked like an idiot, Madhar. What did you do to me?"

"Oh, don't worry, the viewers have nothing to compare you to. They think the galaxy is full of Jim Ables now."

"How embarrassing."

"Hey, I've got some news for you!" continued the slightly inebriated Turcanian.

"What's that?"

"I've done a deal, and I've cut you in for half of the profits!"

"Uh-oh, what deal? It'd better be legal!"

"Absolutely. No question. I just signed a contract with the biggest toy maker. They're going to put out a model construction kit of your craft. It'll be huge! You're in for half the profits, straight. I'll open a *legitimate* bank account for you."

"Wait a minute, Turcanian kids are going to think this heap of crap is cool?"

"You've got it. It's going to be great for the space program. It'll set the bar so low for what our ships have to look like!"

Then, silence on the other end.

"Still there, Madhar?"

"Yes. I was just struck by something."

"What?"

"You said we're Turcanians."

"Yeah?"

"I guess we didn't know that."

Jim replied after a moment. "Don't you have a word for yourselves?"

"No. We have a word for every subfaction and quasi philosophy, but there's no word for *everybody*...except 'everybody.' But that would include you."

"You want to invent one?"

"Oh no, that's not my place. Wait though! Maybe we do have a word."

"What is it?"

"In the old days—I mean centuries ago—they used 'A'nir.' It was used in poems and songs. It was used to describe our ancestors looking up at an eclipse. It has connotations of 'everyone under a shadow,' that sort of thing. You're right; maybe we'd better invent a new one."

THE FILE, PART TWO

Office of External Affairs
Department of Extra-Solar Activities

CONFIDENTIAL

C1 – 032 – TURCANIS MAJOR – Techno-transfer

Assigned to: James Able

Additional documents added pending agent Able's return. Liz

CONFIDENTIAL

Internal Memo
Office of External Affairs

From: Michaelo Korvanotualli

To: Elizabeth Curacao

August 6, 2199

Re: Turcanis Major

Liz,

Questions are being asked about your sending Jim Able to Turcanis.

I understand he is still under medical supervision after the Ch'Garrat affair. I need to have your justification for this. I'm sure he's an accomplished operative, but under the circumstances please let me know your reasoning.

Mike

Internal Memo
Office of External Affairs

From: Elizabeth Curacao

To: Michaelo Korvanotualli

August 6, 2199

Re: Turcanis Major

Mike,

Jim Able is under regular counseling, as are fifteen of our other agents. It's tough out there, as you well remember. He is not under medical treatment per se. I felt he needed a short assignment to get him back on form.

I am currently running a full house with our major projects. Calling Jim back was the only alternative to forgetting about Turcanis.

I have full confidence in Jim's abilities to handle a simple Second Contact visit.

Liz

[Received September 9, 2199 O1#A1-2811]
[Prioritized O1#EC-4293]

From: Patrol Commandant Ngell Amarno, Hawkins
Array, HH Neb.

To: Elizabeth Curacao, OEA, Dept. EA

September 9, 2199

GB5478 – Confirmed sighting of Turcanian

This notice is additional to my prior transmission.

The Turcanian trader whom I identified in February
this year is once more active about this station.

Navigation Controller Hardy identified his flier in
station-keeping eight thousand miles above our
nominal elliptic.

The pilot has tried on several occasions to contact
the criminal Melha Melha.

If you wish I will initiate contact. Please advise.

P.Comm. Amarno

[Outgoing September 11, 2199 O1#B5-2400]

From: Elizabeth Curacao, OEA, Dept. EA

To: Patrol Commandant Ngell Amarno, Hawkins Array, Horsehead Nebula

September 11, 2199

Re: Turcanian trader

Please continue to monitor the Turcanian's activities. There is no need to initiate contact.

We are waiting for the return of our agent from a second contact visit. We will review the situation after a full analysis of this visit.

Thank you for your diligence in this matter, it is much appreciated.

Liz Curacao

[Received September 10, 2199 O1#A1-5231]
[Prioritized 01#EC-4300]

From: Patrol Commandant Ngell Amarno, Hawkins Array, Horsehead Nebula

To: Elizabeth Curacao, OEA, Dept. EA

September 10, 2199

GB5677 – Military Hardware theft from Theta-Proxima

We have secured the Birritan cargo ship, damaged in the attack on the TP training base.

We are currently performing an inventory of the hardware aboard the vessel. I will advise upon completion.

P.Comm. Amarno

[Received September 14, 2199 O1#A1-2661]
[Prioritized O1#EC-4200]

From: Patrol Commandant Ngell Amarno, Hawkins Array, HH Neb.

To: Elizabeth Curacao, OEA, Dept. EA

September 14, 2199

GB5478 – Turcanian Trader

The Turcanian trader has left this area.

P.Comm. Amarno

[Received September 10, 2199 O1#A1-5231]
[Prioritized 01#EC-4300]

From: Patrol Commandant Ngell Amarno, Hawkins Array, Horsehead Nebula

To: Elizabeth Curacao, OEA, Dept. EA

September 10, 2199

GB5677 – Military Hardware theft from Theta-Proxima

We have performed an inventory of the hardware on the Birritan cargo ship.

I regret to inform you that the current contents do not match the expected contents in that the following items were NOT FOUND:

1)	1 (one) lasercannon mounting kit	(65 of 66 found)
2)	1 (one) lasercannon control unit	(65 of 66 found)
3)	1 (one) lasercannon servo-extender kit	(65 of 66 found)
4)	1 (one) lasercannon training pack	(65 of 66 found)
5)	2 (two) lasercannon maintenance packs	(64 of 66 found)
6)	1 (one) Bahstu Corp. Variable G-j lasercannon	(65 of 66 found)
7)	2 (two) Bahstu Corp. Scanner Interface modules	(33 of 35 found)
8)	1 (one) Mobile converter pack	(19 of 20 found)
9)	1 (one) Bahstu Corp. Cannon Carriage	(19 of 20 found)

It may be assumed that these items were removed from the cargo ship prior to the inventory.

P.Com Amarno

Memo from Office of External Affairs

From: Elizabeth Curacao, OEA, Dept. EA

To: Section Chief Tomkins, EIA

September 15, 2199

Re: Prohibited Technology Alert

Attached is an informational from the HH Neb, with ref to the TP training base attack.

Please upgrade GB5677 to a full PTA.

The first person I would like you to try to eliminate from your investigation is the Turcanian. Please cross-reference with the informationals received for GB5478.

Liz

[Received September 18, 2199 01#A1-5231]

[Prioritized Copy to 01#EC-4440]

[Header redacted]

From: Field Agent R546

To: Section Chief Tomkins, EIA.

September 18, 2199

Re: Prohibited Technology Alert 3590 TP Training Base

Initial investigation completed.

Confirmed supply of prohibited equipment to Turcanian.

Confirmed criminal charges to be pursued against Police Officer Arranda Pilo.

Awaiting instructions as to follow-up with Turcanian authorities.

R546

CHAPTER EIGHT

Jim was relieved when he finally returned the flier to the rental agency.

Before long, he was listening to the happy talk of his fellow shuttle passengers. The little old lady next to him watched the disk of the Earth fill the window.

She smiled and said, "There's no place like home. Isn't that what they say?"

"Sure," he replied with a sigh.

Her eyes darted up to his face and away again. "Ah, not born here?"

"Yeah, I was born here, but I grew up on a station."

"And that's home for you? I understand. As long as you have somewhere. It's so important to have roots, don't you think?"

Jim had grown so accustomed to traveling for the OEA from station to station, from planet to planet, that he had long since lost that feeling of connection. Having roots wasn't something he worried about. Earth was special only in that it was the world his parents had known.

"I travel a lot," he said as if to excuse himself. "I'm with the OEA. I'm going back to the office for a while."

"My son works in an office in the city as well. You're too young, of course, to remember what it was like before the place was built."

"You remember them building Unity City?"

"Oh yes, I am that old!" She smiled, and her eyes sparkled at him, but then she frowned. "Beautiful islands, they were...beautiful."

Jim wondered if she would say more. He said, "I remember being taught that UC was humankind's first great gesture. The first thing we ever did all together."

"Hmph! Concrete and steel where there had been sand and palm trees. It was business as usual; that's all."

"I guess you're right. It's a god-awful place to live, same as any other city."

Jim's mind turned to having to face his boss once more. Part of the reason for his constant travel was the difficult relationship he had with Elizabeth Curacao.

The campus of the OEA was one of many that made up the well-ordered network of Unity City. Once his shuttle landed at the spaceport, he took the short train ride to the office.

Jim got as far as the front desk, stopping to chat with the young women placed to protect the office from the public. He wanted to make sure they still remembered him.

"Oh Jim, there's a message for you," said the older, more senior Anne. She read, "'See Liz as soon as you get in.'"

A voice came from the entrance to the main corridor to his right. "That's all right, Anne! I saw him first."

Jim turned and glanced at Liz long enough to confirm that she wasn't pleased to have him back.

Liz wore her hair bleached almost to white. It was cropped into a shape that left no hint of femininity. Her suit, however, was precisely tailored to emphasize her figure. The general impression matched the rumor of the office: that she had been manufactured rather than grown.

Jim winked at Anne and said, "See you later."

"Good luck," she whispered.

"Hi, Liz! Good to be back."

"What the hell were you doing out there? Your Turcanian's procured some serious hardware this time!"

"What?"

She held the door open and flicked her head to order him through. They walked half the length of the enormous open-plan floor—with Liz in front and Jim a respectful three paces behind, in the wake of her frosty silence.

Several faces appeared above partitions as they walked by only to duck down when they saw who was passing.

Reaching his cubicle, she gestured to his chair. "Sit down. Read this. I want you back out there, and I want this sorted!"

She threw the folder down on the desk. "Oh, and make sure you spend a double session with Doctor Dawkins before you leave." She turned and strode away.

Jim congratulated himself on not transmitting the full version of his report while he was en route. It looked like the less she knew right now, the better.

Jim thought back to his early days with the department when he learned how to selectively report the facts until a full revelation could no longer do any harm. He had learned from a master. Robin Stuart could take five times as long on a mission as anyone could have imagined possible, spend the equivalent of a small departmental budget, and cause economic and social havoc on an alien world. He would then submit a draft report saying how well it had all gone and what a pleasant place it was for a visit. He had taught Jim the principle of "temporal refraction."

"Your temp'ral refraction, Jim," he'd say, "is the principle that stops your boss noticing how important something is simply by hiding it sufficiently far back in the past so that other, more recent, things seem far more important in comparison."

In practice, this meant the longer the delay between the draft report and the one with the truth in it, the less trouble that followed. Better yet would be to time the delivery of the report so that the whole department was in the middle of some major crisis, or someone else had just been found involved in some incredibly embarrassing fiasco; the bigger the current mess, the greater the temporal refraction.

He looked at the new pages in the file, some already creased at the edges. He smiled at the old-fashioned way his boss did things. He knew the real reason Liz kept things on paper: you can't slam something electronic down on someone's desk and stalk away. If that weren't enough, she was also an expert at giving her staff instructions, written in pencil, in the margins of printed pages, as separated from the electronic record as if they were in another dimension—untraceable, unattributable, and, above all, completely deniable.

He read through the file.

"Okay," he said quietly to himself. "What are you up to, 'Edward of Turcania'?" He sat back in his chair and put his feet up on the desk. "Are you really going to start a war? I'm sure you're not so mad at the audnir that you're going to zap them— even if they did breach the Agreement of Rubaw or whatever it was."

He listened to the hum of office noise around him for a moment, picked up his stress ball, and began to throw it against his document cabinet and catch it with alternating hands.

"Welcome back, Jim!" came a voice from beyond the partition at the side of his desk.

"Hi, Marty! How you been?"

"Good! You?"

"Fine. Been out eating worms."

"Ooh, I've warned you about that alien food. Bring back any toxic viruses?"

"Not that they can tell."

"Can I have that antique roadster of yours when you die?"

"No. They'll have to burn everything I've ever touched."

"Oh yeah. Right!"

Jim turned over the pages again. He frowned at the list of equipment. This was, indeed, serious hardware. He went over in his mind what he knew of Sopha Luca. Taking out a pencil, he made some notes on the back of one of the memos.

▭

He's methodical.
Dedicated.
Wants to clean Mainworld.
Vaporize trash?

▭

Could it be that simple? He laughed. *What a neat way around the problem of landing there and violating the taboo! He could sit in orbit and do it all from a distance.*

Jim put down his feet and turned to his desk's access terminal. Within a few minutes he was reviewing the capabilities of the Bahstu Corporation's variable gigajoule laser cannon. If Sopha wasn't careful, he would remove the trash, sterilize the soil, and boil rocks meters deep. Even then, the particulates and toxins given off would be a nasty cloud to throw into the atmosphere.

But Sopha would read the instructions as carefully as though they were part of Regdenir Holy Scripture. He would probably give lessons in the use of the laser cannon, sitting proudly in his ornate chair, his blue-cloaked students hanging on every word.

Jim laughed a little, thinking how well Sopha had maneuvered his way through the criminal stratum of the Hawkins Array to buy a contraband device. He found himself impressed by the alien's astuteness.

Jim wanted to talk to Madhar Nect about this. He missed her. There was something comfortable about the squeaky-voiced scientist. It was rare to connect so well with an alien.

He scanned through his abbreviated report on the second contact meetings. It gave, more or less, an account of things that Madhar would have recognized. It mentioned nothing of Beauty. It said nothing about hostages or rescues. It gave a brief overview of the Regdenir. He felt a little guilty in dismissing them so perfunctorily. It was a comfort to know that most Turcanians would have thought it fair and appropriate.

He got up and went to see Liz. She kept him waiting outside her office door for several minutes; she rarely missed an opportunity to reinforce who was boss.

"Ready to go?" she asked.

"Not yet. But maybe we can do this remotely. We just need to confirm a few details with one of my contacts on TMV-One."

"How are you going to do that?"

"I left a relay node in orbit of TMV. We can use that."

"Did they give you permission to do that?"

"No."

Liz sighed and put her head on her hand, in what Jim thought was a studied pose.

"Jim, I've talked to you before about this sort of thing. We have procedures that are there to be followed. We have to ask the local government *before* we install anything in their space!"

"I know they won't mind."

"Damn them! *I* mind."

"Their approach is—they're very reasonable people. Perhaps you should come out and meet them?"

Liz's eyes narrowed. "That is not an option."

Jim knew it wasn't, which is why he liked to remind her occasionally. Along with good advice, Robin Stuart had left him a file of information on several of his superiors. A problem on an offworld mission had forced Liz to fly a desk. The first time he had hinted to her that he knew something about it had been the moment of irrevocable souring between them.

She sighed. "Very well. Activate the node. Give me a full—that is a *full*—report."

Jim smiled and went to book a session with Dawkins.

When he got back from the counselor, Jim spent several hours preparing for his conversation with Madhar Nect—longer, he felt, than he had before they first met.

The good doctor had seemed impatient with him, apparently expecting him to have finished with the sessions. That he had come away carrying a small card made him suspect that Dawkins was managing to get to him somehow after all. It was the sort of gimmick that he usually hated. It had a slogan on each side, written in small red lettering that glittered as you twisted it in the light. It was cheap and gaudy.

I GIVE MYSELF PERMISSION TO FAIL.
I GIVE MYSELF PERMISSION TO SUCCEED.

"Okay," he said as he sat preparing, "which will it be today?"

He assembled a list of questions for the Turcanian. At best, she would agree with the idea that Sopha was harmless and give him enough extra data to flesh out his report. At worst, she would become alarmed, and Jim would have to go to Liz and ask for help tracking down Sopha and stopping him.

Satisfied that he was ready, he put through the call.

"This is Nect."

"Greetings, Madhar Nect, this is Jim Able."

"Greetings, Jim Able! Are you back so soon?"

"No, I'm on Earth. I have rigged up a patch into your system. How's the quality? Can you hear me okay?"

"Yes, fine. This is amazing. Is this technology you can sell us?"

"Ah...not personally, but I'm sure it would be possible."

"Great, this is great."

"Is everything going all right?"

"Yes. The elections are over—for a short while at least."

"Did the conservatives lose like you thought?"

"Oh yes, big time. Everyone's on the space bandwagon now."

"Congratulations."

"Mixed blessing. There's a lot of tree climbing going on. People who can't even add are trying to pretend to be science policy makers. It's nothing unusual for us."

"Madhar, have you had any news about Sopha Luca?"

"No. Why would I?"

"He's out and about again."

"Oh no! That was some ship he had. Made yours look like a tin bucket."

"I know. Listen, Madhar. I need to ask you about what he's up to. Can you spend a few minutes with me?"

"Of course. For my business partner, all the time you want!"

"I appreciate it. Sopha Luca has bought a laser cannon."

"What's a laser cannon, Jim?"

"A weapon. A military attack weapon." Jim heard Madhar sigh deeply. "My guess is he's going to use it to vaporize the remains of your spacecraft sitting on the surface of Mainworld."

Madhar laughed. "Jim, did you say vaporize?"

"Yes. It will effectively burn them into a gas."

"Neat trick. Can we buy these things too?"

"No, strictly prohibited. You have to invent them yourselves."

"Hah! I knew there was a catch to this somewhere."

"In fact, this one is stolen property. The guy who sold it to him is already in jail."

The scientist asked, "How did Sopha Luca learn about these things?"

"I don't know...Well, maybe I told him."

"Uh-oh."

"Yeah. I told him about their use in surgical operations—small ones. But I guess he realized the possibilities for what he wanted."

"Hmm. He's sharp, that's for sure."

"Sharp enough to realize what he's got, once he's cleaned up Mainworld?"

"What do you mean?"

"What happens when you have to send in helicopters to get him next time? He'll be able to burn them out of the sky."

Madhar used one of the expletives Jim had wanted to learn from her. After a pause, the scientist continued with a slight shake in her voice. "With a weapon like that, he could set up a throne in orbit and become king of the world. Jim, we have to stop him!"

"Yeah. See why I'm calling? Do you think he's likely to stop at being a cleaner?"

"I'm a scientist, Jim, not a psychologist."

Jim hesitated, turning the card from his therapist over in his hand: I GIVE MYSELF PERMISSION TO FAIL. I GIVE MYSELF PERMISSION TO SUCCEED.

"I'm probably going to regret this, but," he continued, "I feel partly responsible for all this. Shall I come back and try and track him down?"

"Oh, it's not your doing. I told you that. You didn't make the Regdenir weird. They did that all on their own. Let me think...Is there any defense against this laser thing?"

"Not much. It depends on the range and the circumstances. I wouldn't like to look up the wrong end of it."

"Then I guess we need some help. He can't be trusted with it, if that's what you're asking. But this is really a government matter now. I can't invite you back in any official capacity. You'll have to be called in by them."

"How easy will that be?"

"It won't be simple. There are plenty of politicians who would love to be the one to bring you back. That's what we call 'a fruit'—something they can say they produced so that people will come back to their 'tree' at election time—you understand?"

"Yeah, I understand. You don't have a department that deals with global threats?"

"No. Well...I say that, but we might have. Who knows? It might be an empty desk somewhere in a government building."

"Madhar, I'll leave it to you. Find me who to talk to. It looks like I'm coming back."

JIM ABLE OFFWORLD

TMV

3

ED CHARLTON

AUTHOR OF "THE ALERONDE TRILOGY"

CHAPTER NINE

"Madhar, I'll leave it to you. Find me who to talk to. It looks like I'm coming back."

"Okay, Jim. It'll be good to see you."

Jim nearly hung up, but he changed his mind.

"Madhar, one more thing, I think..."

"Go ahead."

"We should perhaps be watching out for Sopha Luca, to see what he does. What state are your astronomers in? I know *you* have a telescope. Are there many more?"

"What did you have in mind?"

"Keeping watch on Mainworld. You'll be looking for unusual flashes or even persistent beams of light. You may see clouds of smoke or particulates. I guess you should concentrate on the old landing site."

"They'd need to be sizeable for us to see them."

"I was afraid of that."

"Bring some better telescopes with you, Jim, as a goodwill gift to the scientists of 'Turcanis.'"

"Maybe. Are you unhappy with that name?"

"Well, it isn't our name. It sounds a bit like a colloquial term for one of the bumps on our heads. Given the peculiarities of your anatomy, I suppose it isn't too bad...to emphasize our distinctiveness."

Jim looked down his list of questions. "Madhar, one more thing."

"Another?"

"Small matter. When your guys explored Mainworld and discovered the Maggnir, what did the Regdenir think of that—of the Maggnir?"

"Oh, I've no idea, not a clue. You'd need to go back to your Regdenir contacts. All I know is the fuss about landing on Mainworld. Can't help you. Maybe they worship the Maggnir too; I wouldn't know."

"Okay. Thanks for all your help."

"How can I use this link of yours? Can I call you?"

"No. It's set up just for me at the moment. I'll call again when I'm on my way. You can definitely get government help?"

"I'll try."

"Madhar, you're a true friend."

"As you are, Jim Able."

Jim wrote a supplement to his report recommending Sopha Luca be allowed to use the laser cannon for his religious purposes. After that, Jim reasoned, the Turcanian might be in a mood to talk about returning the weapon. He wanted to have something in the report that gave the impression he knew what he was doing. He saw no need to mention Madhar's fears.

He decided not to send the report electronically. He printed a paper copy and went to see his boss.

She was in a meeting with someone Jim did not recognize. In fact, the visitor was a species he did not recognize. The plain fact of an alien visiting the OEA was strange enough. That Liz should be hosting one was astonishing.

"Jim!" she called from inside her office. "Come in."

He walked into the office and caught the eye of the alien. Its head bowed slightly in greeting, but it said nothing.

"Good morning," said Jim politely. He had intended to place the report firmly on her desk, but she stood and took it from him before he could get the chance.

"Please take a seat."

He was taken off guard. Not knowing what was happening was common enough out on an assignment; it was disorientating for it to happen in the office.

While she read his report, he took a long sideways look at the alien in the chair next to him. It was a slender primate about seven feet tall, wearing a single plain, seamless piece of clothing with a half-hood covering the back of its head. Black leather boots showed below; they seemed somehow wider than a human would need.

The alien's skin caught Jim's attention more than its clothing; he couldn't work out the color. Where an arm rested on the wooden part of the chair, the skin seemed to be light brown and wrinkled, but its face was smooth and white like its robe. As the alien lifted an arm to stroke the back of its head, the arm immediately lost its brown color, the wrinkles becoming smooth and pale. Out of the corner of his eye, Jim saw the color and texture change back as the arm made contact once more with the wood of the chair.

A chameleon? he wondered. He had never heard of an intelligent species with that ability.

The alien's face was also unexpected. It was smooth-skinned with a small nose. The eyes were small and seemed flush with the brow and cheeks. It was an impassive, unrevealing face.

Liz looked up from the report. "I think your recommendation is dangerous in the extreme." To his surprise, she handed the report to the alien. "This is Tella, from the External Intelligence Agency. The information on the Turcanian's recent acquisitions came from Tella's work."

Jim was learning a great deal this morning. The EIA employed non-humans! This was the sort of thing that brought down governments. He knew that a band of EIA operatives had only code names on their correspondence. Their identity was always supposed to be closely guarded. Now he knew why. But why was he being introduced to one?

He turned to the alien and held out his hand, saying, "Pleased to meet you, Tella." Tella took his hand, and Jim saw the alien's skin blush pink in a reflection of Jim's own.

"Jim. I have read your reports on Turcanis Major."

The alien's voice was modulated such that Jim got no clue as to its sex. The noncommittal greeting gave him no clue as to whether Tella was friend or foe. Liz smiled at Jim, an enigmatic smile that further unsettled him.

"Tella has been given the task of retrieving the stolen hardware. You will provide all necessary assistance."

"You know," Jim said to both Tella and Liz, "that the Turcanian thinks he is the legitimate owner now? He believes he bought the stuff fair and square."

"I doubt that," said Liz. "I think he will know very well the merchandise was hot. He didn't get it from a store."

"I know, but...," Jim responded.

Tella interrupted. "I know how the sale was made. It was a secret rendezvous. It was a secret exchange. It had been arranged at a private meeting. Is this how business is performed on Turcanis Major Five-One?"

"Who knows? Sometimes it may be. If the seller didn't tell Sopha that the stuff was stolen, I don't imagine he would think to ask."

"Would he have cared?" asked Liz.

Jim hesitated. "No. I don't think anything would stop him. He is a...dedicated individual."

"An obsessive nutcase," Liz suggested.

"*You* might think so," Jim said, a little more harshly than he meant.

Tella's head turned from one to the other in the silence that followed, the impassive pale face graying slightly.

Liz stood up. "Consider yourself part of Tella's team. Bring back the hardware."

The meeting was over.

As they stood outside, Jim looked up at Tella. "What's the plan, boss?"

Tella smiled, the thin pale lips barely distinguishable. "Plan?"

"Yes, what do we do first?"

"Ah, first we eat lunch. Then tonight we meet and get drunk. Tomorrow we take our hangovers to Turcanis Major Five-One. Will that suffice?"

Jim laughed out loud. "Oh my! You read my thoughts."

It was at lunch that Jim learned the basic facts about Tella. The inhabitants of Tella's homeworld referred to it as Neraff. The chameleon characteristics marked Tella as a part of a persecuted subspecies. The majority on Neraff were physically similar but remained almost colorless. Tella had been working for the EIA for three years, after an indeterminate period spent hitchhiking through space.

Near the end of the meal in the OEA canteen, Jim finally got around to the question foremost on his mind.

"Tella, excuse me, but are you male or female?"

Tella's eyes narrowed. "That is not a question you may ask without giving offense."

"Oh...sorry. But how do I introduce you? Do I say 'This is Tella, *he's* from Neraff' or '*she's* from Neraff'?"

"No. You may say 'This is Tella, from Neraff.' Nothing more is required."

"Well, I may get that wrong sometimes. Don't be upset; it's not something I'm used to."

"I understand. In our first years of contact with other races, that matter was one that caused much misunderstanding. I am familiar with the problems that other races have in thinking in different terms."

Jim was not sure if this partnership was going to work. As he prepared for the evening, he kept wondering if he was going out on a date.

Alcohol seemed to affect the Neraffan the same way it did Jim. Tella could match him drink for drink, stupid bar game for stupid bar game. They spent long periods of the evening exaggerating tales of appalling alien food and its disastrous effects on their digestive systems. All evening Jim saw that whatever came close to, or in contact with, the alien's skin had its color reflected back in a delicate dance. At one point, demonstrating the active nature of its skin's ability, Tella held up a tall amber beer, and its hand glowed with a similar hue. To Jim's amusement, small pale dots ran up the hand, paralleling the bubbles rising in the glass.

Jim never could remember the end of the evening. The journey to the spaceport the next morning was long, loud, and painful.

Tella met him at the terminal and took him through an unmarked door, where a security team was waiting.

"Welcome to the world of the EIA, Jim," said Tella. They were ushered through various scanners and into the secure terminal.

"Aren't we renting a commercial flier?"

"I'm not allowed to travel in commercial vehicles. I can only use agency fliers."

"Oh. It avoids questions, I suppose."

"It allows me to be insured. Earth-owned companies still discriminate against aliens. The courts may soon intervene, but until then, I am restricted in many things."

"I didn't realize."

They were led to a departure gate. As Jim saw the agency flier through the window, his mind immediately turned to his business interests on TMV-I.

"The toy makers are going to love this!"

"Would you repeat that?" asked Tella.

"Oh...nothing. I'll explain later."

The flier was from the same exclusive ship maker as Sopha's. It had several suspicious bulges—perhaps covering scanners, perhaps concealing weapons.

Tella watched as Jim admired the machine. "It is a PR555 stealth flier. It has full covert-operation capabilities. It is also very fast." The Neraffan smiled. "Will it do?"

"Oh yes, this will do. Can you fly it?"

"Maybe."

Jim smiled in return. He had no doubt that his new friend was quite able to handle such a machine.

Jim and Tella did not go directly to Turcanis Major. Tella insisted that they go first to the Horsehead Nebula. Jim's protests that they were wasting two days of travel in each direction held no sway.

Jim had never been to the Horsehead Nebula, but he had heard bad things about it. A large trading post had grown up around the Hawkins Array. No one had planned it, and the authorities had apathetically watched it happen. Businesses would open up by docking alongside existing structures and negotiating passage through each other's modules for customers and stock. It had become a labyrinth of odd-sized compartments and walkways. Older businesses became frozen in place by the concessions and contracts as unchangeable as the positions of docking clamps and open airlocks. Various sections had become derelict—dark holes kept serviceable by neighbors motivated solely by the fear of atmospheric leaks. As with any community, the bigger it got, the more people came. With people came the need for a large police unit. If he hadn't had to, Jim would have gone nowhere near it.

Tella arranged with the patrol commandant for Jim to interview the rogue police officer who had sold the stolen equipment to Sopha Luca.

"I will be there to observe him. You know the questions to ask because you know Sopha. I know what to look for because I know criminals."

Jim didn't think it necessary but said, "Whatever you say, Tella. We can give it a try."

Tella docked the flier at one of the police unit's own bays. These were secure from the rest of the station and had been constructed to be out of the line of sight of any windows.

Patrol Commandant Ngell Amarno seemed excited to see Tella again. Jim was introduced but, he felt, otherwise ignored.

"I'm cut up about Arranda Pilo. I liked him," Amarno began. "He had a great rapport with the traders. He had their confidence.

His work made my life a whole lot easier. He had a damn good future. But he went native. It's always a risk. He'll be going to Earth at the end of the month. I've told them I can't accommodate him any longer than that. I think they would rather not bother. Anything special you need?"

Tella shook its head slowly. "The usual—no one is to mention me, and I get into the room well ahead of Pilo."

"I don't understand...," began Jim, but Tella interrupted.

"You will. Just pretend that you are interviewing Pilo as part of *your* investigation of the Turcanian. That's all."

Jim frowned but said, "Okay."

He waited in Amarno's office while Tella was shown to the interview room. The desk was neat and the office tidy. Jim appreciated the skill it must take to keep order in such a chaotic environment.

"Okay, Mr. Able, we're ready for you," said the commandant as he held open the door. "Please follow me."

Jim followed him down a corridor and then down a narrow ladder into what must have been an added external module. The temperature had dropped, and the light was poor. Jim felt like he was suddenly aboard a submarine.

Amarno opened the door of the interview room and stood back. A single light shone on the prisoner seated at a small table. There was no sign of Tella.

"You are former police officer Arranda Pilo?" Jim began.

"You know it," he said without looking at Jim.

"I am James Able of the Office of External Affairs. I would like you to go over the circumstances of the trade with the Turcanian."

"Who?"

Jim opened his folder on the table and turned around a picture of Sopha Luca.

"The Turcanian."

Pilo snorted and looked at the floor. "It's already been written up. You don't need any more."

"I do. I need to know about this guy. I'd like to stop him before he injures himself or someone else with his purchase."

Pilo looked up at Jim briefly before silently returning his gaze to the floor.

"Why did he want it?" asked Jim.

"He didn't say."

"Did he have a shopping list, or did you give him a catalog to browse through?"

Pilo did not answer.

"Let's try it this way," said Jim, sighing. "He's nosing about looking for a trader called Melha Melha. You hear he's in the market for some stuff. What was the very first thing he asked for? How did he describe it?"

"I don't remember."

"Try. It could help."

"Help you or me?"

"I can't stop your being sent back to Earth, but I can recommend reasonable treatment. I'm with the OEA, not the magistrates."

Pilo crossed his arms and half-turned away from Jim. "I don't remember."

"Did he say he wanted something to melt metal?"

Pilo frowned and said, "No."

Jim heard the implied *Don't be ridiculous.*

"So what was it?"

"I told you; I don't remember."

"Did he say he was looking for military hardware?"

"No."

"Come on, Arranda. How did he express it to you?"

"What do you care?" snapped the ex-officer.

"It matters. Lives could be at stake."

"So?"

Jim sighed. He hated this stuff. Guys who were already convicted lost all perspective. Their lives disintegrated into black-and-white issues of survival. He felt this wasn't going to be productive. He waited for a long while and started to doodle on his notepad.

He was thinking of Sopha's ambition. He drew a circle with a small "x" in it, then another circle with another "x"—one for Mainworld and one for its largest moon. He drew a thin line from one to the other.

"So what did he ask you? How did he describe what he wanted?" he asked without looking at Pilo.

Pilo sighed. "Yeah."

"'Yeah,' what?"

"Yeah, that was it."

"What was?"

Pilo nodded towards Jim's notepad.

"Like that. That's like what he drew. He had angles, distances, size of target. He didn't know the technicalities, but he had the math down."

"Details."

Pilo shook his head. "I don't remember. He kept the drawings. I knew he'd need a major piece. The distance...through an atmosphere...that small a target. Had to be major."

"How small?"

"Two meters."

Jim wrote it down.

"Oh, and it had to be linked to an IR scanner. He was dead keen on that. I guess he'd already set up the targeting through the scanner; he just needed the delivery."

Jim could imagine more of the conversation now. He could picture Sopha slowly describing what he meant, using the picture as a guide. It seemed to be reasonable. Pilo was telling the truth.

"Did he ask anything about discharges, environmental effects, toxic residues—that kind of thing?"

"Yeah, he asked—but I didn't tell him. I sold him the books. He could read."

"What do you think his target was?"

"Don't know, don't care." Pilo was silent and looking at the floor again. "He just said 'the scar.'"

"'The scar'?"

"Yeah, that's what he said. He said he was performing surgery to remove a scar."

Jim stroked his cheek. Pilo looked into the distance. "But, then, he said 'scars.' One time he said 'scars.'"

"Definitely plural?"

"I'd been wondering how much he would spend on something he was only going to fire once. Once he said 'scars,' I knew it wasn't a one-off. Then I knew I had him."

Jim frowned. Pilo sounded truthful, but Jim thought he had probably misunderstood the Turcanian. He imagined Sopha repeatedly firing the laser to scour the entire landing site to remove what he and his religious order felt was a blasphemy. Madhar Nect's people had left parts of a landing-relaunch vehicle on their Mainworld. "Did you go over details like recharge times?"

"Like I said, he had the books."

Jim rapidly asked the other questions he and Tella had prepared. Pilo was talking freely now. Within a few more minutes, the interview was over, and Jim pressed a buzzer for Amarno to come back in. Jim thanked Pilo for his help but was met with a hostile squint.

After Pilo was led out, Jim sighed deeply and heard a sound behind him. Turning quickly, he saw the plain wall of the interview room move. A faint ripple in the paintwork moved along the top of a cupboard and picked up a white robe. Tella became visible once more as it took on the reflection of its clothing.

"That went well, Jim, very well."

"I...I'm glad. I'm also amazed that you can do that."

"I don't advertise it. I don't want people thinking that I like loitering naked in dark corners."

Jim laughed. "No, I suppose not."

Jim and Tella left the Hawkins Array shortly after the interview. Tella had learned enough.

"Sopha Luca does not know the device was stolen," Tella said as they settled into their flier.

"You sure?"

"Absolutely. For Sopha, Pilo was an official. He would have played up that aspect to gain Sopha's trust."

"How do you know that?"

"I know from watching him and from listening to his breathing as he spoke with you. It is always revealing."

"Really?"

"Pilo is an excellent salesman. He will probably work the prison system to his advantage. Once he realizes that he can still sell things, he will quickly rise."

Jim shook his head. He had assessed Pilo as a loser.

When they had traveled far enough to engage the autopilot, Tella turned to Jim.

"Now, tell me again about Sopha's religious beliefs that have brought him to this point. Why does he want to clean all foreign matter from TMV?"

Jim thought back to the night on the promontory. He remembered how inspiring it had been. He sighed. "Do you know who Albert Einstein was?"

"No."

"Well, he was one of our greatest thinkers and scientists. He once said that a great unanswered question is whether the universe is friendly."

Tella smiled and looked at Jim. "That is a very excellent question. I am surprised to hear it from a human."

Jim frowned but let the remark pass. "The Turcanians, well, the Regdenir anyway, have an answer to it. The planet is very beautiful when seen from their moon. They...pivot their beliefs on that. They believe that because the universe contains something beautiful, well...then it isn't so bad. It changes how they look at the rest of the universe. Sopha said that because there is beauty, there is room for love and hope, and so on."

Tella did not immediately reply.

"You really need to see it, and to hear a Regdenir talk about it." Jim shook his head. "I'm not expressing it well."

Tella lifted a pale hand. "You have said enough."

They were both silent for a while. Then Tella said, "It is a profound belief. It is an insight that many would miss. We have a responsibility here."

"What's that?"

"This insight, this belief...we must do nothing that would cause it to be lost to the universe."

Jim wondered if he understood Tella's implication. "I should hope not. Liz has already told me not to start a war. I have no intention of allowing any harm to come to anyone."

"No, you misunderstand me. I mean this." Tella was silent and still, then continued, "The others, the 'audnir,' do not share the belief, yet it will be these who venture out into the galaxy. Turcanis will become whatever they make it in the eyes of other races. The beliefs of the Regdenir will be...overlooked. Who will come to listen to the Regdenir? Who will hear of them? Those who do will hear nothing good of them. Do you begin to understand?"

Tella was silent again for a long time before speaking. "Our responsibility is to hold the door open to both Regdenir and audnir; they may not be ready, they may not care. We must court both sides, Jim. What do you think?"

Jim had not expected such thinking from his strange colleague. "I don't think they'll care. To them, we are all audnir. They will want nothing to do with us. As Madhar said, they have made themselves weird. There's nothing we can do about it."

"They are precious because their insights are precious. We must treat them with proactive respect. They hold an idea. We must hold them up because of it."

"'Don't throw the baby out with the bathwater,' you mean?"

"A most curious expression." The pale smile spread across Tella's face. "But, yes. There is a 'baby' there. It is a good image."

There was another long silence until Tella spoke again. "The audnir spacecraft left remains on this most beautiful world. But the Regdenir have never been there to see how bad the damage is. It might already have been overgrown or absorbed into the soil. The world may have already repaired the damage."

"I hadn't thought of that."

"And if he reads the documentation with his purchase, he may find the effects of his work to be far worse than the present state."

"He will have read it, but I wonder if his science is strong enough to realize the full implications."

"Is Sopha open to discussion and reasoned argument?"

Jim laughed. "Discussion and argument are a way of life for them. They have discussions that last for generations. Do you mean 'Will he change his mind?' I think the answer is no."

Tella made no answer, but Jim got the impression of a slight darkening in his colleague's skin tone.

CHAPTER TEN

A few days later, Tella and Jim began to plan in detail their work on TMV-I.

"We can meet with Madhar Nect easily enough. She said she would try to arrange a meeting with the government."

"Yes, we should begin as officially as possible," said Tella, nodding.

"Perhaps we should call her?"

"Soon. Which Regdenir have you chosen to visit?"

"I...I haven't. I don't really know any others. I corresponded with a few, but they are very closed."

Tella looked at Jim with no discernible expression.

"They don't have the kind of parties that I get invited to," Jim joked.

"Perhaps we should throw one ourselves?"

"What? Are you kidding?"

"No. I am serious. We should encourage them. We could invite them to meet us, since we are doing the same for the government. Perhaps we could even have some sort of sharing of food or entertainment—something to help them feel comfortable with us?"

"How? Where?"

"This you must know. Where can we land in the Regdenir area?"

"There's one good place. Where Sopha met me."

"Then that is clear. The choice then is *whom* to invite."

"I'll think about it," said Jim, shaking his head. He felt his relationship with Tella was only progressing in fits and starts. It was bad enough working for Liz, who did not think the same way he did, but working for someone he had to refer to as "it," and who had a truly alien mind was, at times, disturbing.

Jim spent the next day reviewing the message traffic he had recorded from Regde99. Tella seemed in a strange mood—not that it involved any change of expression, merely a withdrawing for long periods into a kind of trance.

Late that night, Tella came alive again. "Now, have you chosen the Regdenir?"

"I guess so. There are two who I think would at least consider an invitation."

"Let us draft the message with care."

"Can't it wait until the morning? I was about to go to sleep."

"Jim, you've done nothing but laze around all day! Come, let's get to work!"

It took three hours before Tella was satisfied with the wording of the message. Jim's only comfort in the process was the thought that Tella could out-nitpick even a Regdenir.

▭

angaraVmyournVregde1Vapp
    dlaviVherucVregde3Vopp

Greetings, Angara Myourn and Dlavi Heruc.

We have corresponded before on the topic of offworld technology. Dlavi Heruc, you were most helpful in our search for Sopha Luca, for which we send thanks.

We now write more openly as James Able of Earth and Tella of Neraff, two visitors from two planets of other stars.

We officially represent the people of Earth and greet you on their behalf.

We will meet shortly with representatives of your world's government and with Madhar Nect, who allows us to use this message-ID.

We wish to meet you as representatives of the Barottin Regdenir.

We believe our visit will not be complete until we meet you, though you may wish to have others meet us in your place.

Our desire to meet with you is based on our appreciation for the antiquity and nobility of your beliefs. We have learned that you treasure Beauty. Perhaps we too may learn something of Beauty by our meeting.

We regret to add that our meeting must also address a serious matter regarding Sopha Luca who, in ignorance and misled by a criminal, has in his possession a stolen machine. This machine could cause injury to Sopha Luca or to others. It is our most urgent desire to avert any harm.

We suggest that our meeting take place at the retreat house used, until recently, by Sopha Luca. It stands at the head of the valley, east of the tallest mountains, in the forest north of Oppudim. We will arrive there on the morning of the third day from now.

g101VnectVlatsinVux

---

g101VnectVlatsinVux

Greetings, James Able of Earth and Tella of Neraff.

Perhaps my heart burns with a proper curiosity, and my desire to meet with visitors from so far is a small part of Beauty.

Then I would need to neglect my duties, and my teachers would have to hold their wisdom until my return.

Alas, this cannot be.

Rest in Beauty at your meeting and on your return to your homes.

dlaviVherucVregde3Vopp

---

g101VnectVlatsinVux

Greetings, James Able and Tella.

Perhaps your first visit to our world was not to your profit.

Perhaps your meeting with Sopha Luca was not enough to satisfy your ambitions.

Then you return to speak with more of us, to find those with views more inclined to your own.

If Sopha Luca has acquired a dangerous machine, be sure to address the matter with Sopha Luca. It is he who knows of such things, not I.

angaraVmyournVregde1Vapp

Jim shook his head.

"I told you this wouldn't be simple. They are so closed."

Tella was silent, reading and rereading the messages.

"We swim in waters that have many currents. There is much unsaid in these words."

"Beats me where we go from here," said Jim.

"He knows about your visit. He knows it did not end well. He knows Sopha Luca is...What was your expression about a cannon?"

"A loose cannon."

"Yes, this he knows also. I think he will meet with us."

Jim laughed. "How can you tell from that flat rejection?"

"By the absence of rejection. This is an obstacle, not a closed door."

---

angaraVmyournVregde1Vapp

Greetings, Angara Myourn.

Perhaps you are correct, and the visit was neither to our profit nor yours.

Perhaps you know much of what transpired during the prior visit of James Able.

Perhaps you know of the attempt of Sopha Luca to imprison James Able to prevent information from being available to Madhar Nect.

Perhaps you know of Sopha Luca's departure in haste from your world.

Then also know that our return signifies no hostility on our part. Our return signifies a desire to overcome the misunderstandings that colored the prior visit.

You realize that, in any early dealings between peoples, misunderstanding gives way to understanding, incomprehension gives way to comprehension, and lack of appreciation of Beauty gives way to appreciation of Beauty.

g101VnectVlatsinVux

---

g101VnectVlatsinVux

Greetings, visitors.

It is not our practice to think of extending our ways to those outside.

Your understanding, your comprehension, your appreciation are matters for yourselves to address. Do not look to the Regdenir for your salvation.

The comings and goings of Sopha Luca are likewise matters for ourselves. We do not look to you for help in this matter.

angaraVmyournVregde1Vapp

Jim threw up his hands in defeat. Tella bent over the monitor, shaking his head.

"Jim, you must think more clearly. There is only one topic of conversation here. Will he meet us or not? This is merely another obstacle; the door is not yet closed."

Jim smiled wryly. He thought Tella would learn otherwise.

"Show me his writings again," said Tella. "I must learn to express things better, even more as he does. This is the game."

They spent several hours reading the correspondence over before Tella tried again.

⬚⬚

angaraVmyournVregde1Vapp

Greetings, Angara Myourn.

Perhaps you are correct, and your most clear and lucid definition of "audnir" is an end to the matter.

Then we are not wise in any regard, and our visit is most foolish. For this truth, that the people of Earth, of Neraff, and the Regdenir are different, that they have different paths to walk, that they have different concerns and responsibilities, this is obvious to all. To learn this, we could have spent but a moment in thought while still resting in our beds and never traveled through the stars.

Unless, of course, it is this difference itself that brings us.

Unless, of course, we know that we do not already possess all knowledge and all wisdom.

Unless, of course, we know that by seeking out others, different from ourselves, we can be enriched where we are lacking, and enrich where we find lack.

If we knew already the outcome before each such meeting, perhaps we would seldom need to travel. But we do not know what will happen when we travel. Angara Myourn, do you?

If in our uncertainty we travel so far, in your certainty how far will you travel?

g101VnectVlatsinVux

⬚⬚

"Now we shall see what this Turcanian is made of!" said Tella, slapping a hand down on the control panel.

"I'm glad you're enjoying this," muttered Jim, yawning.

———

g101VnectVlatsinVux

Greetings, visitors.

Perhaps you are correct, and I am corrected.

Then our ways are flawed, and for uncounted centuries we have been unknowingly crippled, awaiting only this chance encounter so that we may lean on your wisdom and your ways to make us whole.

Unless, of course, it is we who know Beauty and you who do not.

Unless, of course, it is we who are whole and you who limp your way from star to star, spreading your distorted vision as you go.

angaraVmyournVregde1Vapp

———

Jim became angry. Tella laughed again.

"He's arguing against what he wrote before!" shouted Jim, dragging his fingers through his hair.

Tella shook his head. "He is arguing. We do not yet see against what or whom."

"I don't get it."

"Remember what you learned about the Regdekol. All their writings are there, all the ideas available to all."

"Yeah, that's about right."

"This correspondence is also taking place within the bounds of the Regdekol."

"But..." Jim caught his breath. "So what?"

"It is not against himself or against us that he argues. He is laying down the philosophical justification for our meeting. They have been isolated for a long time. They need to remember that it is permissible to deal with the audnir. He is already convinced, but he must not seem to be acting individually. He needs a theoretical basis for his actions."

"And he wants us to provide it."

"If we cannot, he cannot. He cannot be seen to have instigated this. He is looking, perhaps, for something specific from us."

▭

angaraVmyournVregde1Vapp

Greetings, Angara Myourn.

Perhaps you are correct, and we are corrected.

Then you are the doctors to whose expertise we must submit and have our vision healed.

Unless, of course, the distortion you diagnose comes not from disease or injury but from the differences in what we have seen.

Is it possible, Angara Myourn, that others have seen Beauty elsewhere?

Is it possible, Regdenir, that you protect and serve but one instance of Beauty and that Beauty is manifest in other places in the universe?

Would this not be a glorious discovery?

Is the chance of this not worth a small consideration?

g101VnectVlatsinVux

▭

g101VnectVlatsinVux

Greetings, visitors.

We have for many centuries lamented the blindness of our audnir. They look where we look, but see it not. They know what we know, and understand it not.

You suggest that you are audnir of a different kind, who do not see what we see and see something we do not, and yet who know what we know and understand what we understand.

That such a differentiation exists between audnir on our world and audnir from other worlds is not an idea with which we are yet comfortable.

As for your claim that Beauty is not unique? I must keep in mind that your voice is neither that of a child nor an audnir of this world nor a heretical Regdenir but a new voice. I should warn you strangers that tongues were burnt out for such words in days past, though I do not believe it is our practice today.

To know if this could be true would require the investigation and analysis of our greatest minds. If this could be true, the Regdenir would face a profound change. This is not a light matter. This is of deep and lasting consequence.

I do not know how best to proceed to investigate such a claim.

My colleagues and I will need to address this matter with all haste.

Continue with your proposal to land at the Berwashe Retreat House until more discussion can take place.

Rest in Beauty.

angaraVmyournVregde1Vapp

———

Tella clapped its hands together. "As you say, Jim, 'Bingo!'"

"Unbelievable. You think we've done it?"

"It is done. He needs only to arrange which of his 'greatest minds' will meet us."

"Do you want to orbit TMV or its moon?" asked Jim as they arrived in the Turcanis Major system.

"The moon. There is no need for secrecy."

"We should find out what Madhar Nect has arranged for us."

Tella nodded. "She should be prepared for me. I fear they will find me more alien than they did you."

Jim nodded. "I'd suggest covering up as much as possible."

"We usually do," Tella replied, and Jim thought he detected a tinge of sadness.

———

madharVnectVlatsinVux

Greetings, Madhar Nect.

We have arrived.

I am here with Tella of Neraff, whose appearance is different from mine, but I know you'll get along fine. How have the arrangements worked out?

Jim Able

g101VnectVlatsinVux

———

g101VnectVlatsinVux

Greetings, Jim Able.

Not good. Things, as I told you, are fluid in our government. Already, three of the officials I talked to have been moved into positions where they can no longer assist us.

Your imminent arrival has fed something of a frenzy. All are looking for the maximum leverage for when trade starts. I don't know that the current administration is strong enough to handle the pressure. I never thought I'd live to see the day I wished for a dictator!

Do not visit me yet. I will continue to work to set up the meetings, but it may take several days.

madharVnectVlatsinVux

———

madharVnectVlatsinVux

Greetings, Madhar Nect.

We are sorry to be the focus of such unfortunate attention.

Under the circumstances, we may have to meet with your Regdenir cousins before we meet your officials. We have set up a session with them tomorrow.

g101VnectVlatsinVux

g101VnectVlatsinVux

Greetings, Jim Able.

I am amazed! After what you went through last time, are you seriously going back? I urge you to wait. With the situation as it is, I can't guarantee your safety. I don't think there would be unanimity in arranging a second rescue. Please don't do anything so foolish!

madharVnectVlatsinVux

madharVnectVlatsinVux

Greetings, Madhar Nect.

Too late—we are committed. I don't think this will have the same kind of outcome. This time we are meeting with Regdel people. We would not go if we thought we were in danger. But just in case, we will be at the same location.

g101VnectVlatsinVux

g101VnectVlatsinVux

Greetings, Jim Able.

Are all alien races so stubborn and unwilling to take advice? I do not have the faith that you show in the good nature of even the Regdel. They are crazy! Do not trust them. Do not go without at least a plan to get out quickly!

madharVnectVlatsinVux

Tella nodded slowly. "Her caution is wise. We will have a remote control for the flier with us at all times." He drew out a compact device from a compartment in the ceiling. He spent several minutes explaining to Jim the main controls. "These are for the weapons. You can see here the targeting parameters."

"That's...That's very dangerous, isn't it?"

"Danger is relative. If we need to activate this system, it means that the danger is imminent and, for some reason, we have lost control of the situation."

"That's not what I meant, and you know it."

"I respect all life, as you do. But I have used this system in an emergency before. It has saved my life. I hope we do not have to activate it."

"Damn right!"

Madhar Nect waited for a while to see if Jim Able would reply to her last warning. She was seated in her office at the Latsin Institute. It was midafternoon, and the teaching day was winding down. The last class was finishing its work in silence in the classroom next door. As soon as they were done, she could make her way to the TV studio for the evening broadcast.

"Madhar Nect?"

The voice came from the door to the corridor. Her visitor was tall and muscular. He wore a thick armored tunic and held a projectile weapon loosely in his hand.

"No, she's in the room down the end."

He hesitated only for a second. "You are Madhar Nect. You will come with me."

"I'm still teaching a class. Who are you?"

"No questions. Come now!" He raised his weapon. As he did so, a young student opened the door from the classroom.

"Professor?"

"Not now, Yura! Can't you see I'm being kidnapped?"

The student froze in shock for only a second as she took in the scene, then she threw herself back into the classroom and slammed the door.

"You must at least tell me who sent you."

"I don't ask questions like that. Nor should you. Move quickly!"

Madhar got up slowly from her desk. She gave a thought to Jim Able. This might complicate things for her friend. As she raised her hands and walked toward her visitor, she could hear her class moving next door. By the time she had stepped into the corridor, it was full of wide-eyed students.

"Move back!" shouted her visitor.

The students froze, and the corridor became silent.

"Or you'll do what?" asked Nect. "You'll kill thirty-five students and me? I don't think that's quite what you were told to do, is it?"

"Make way and no one will get hurt!"

"No, my ignorant friend, that isn't how we do things here. You will place your weapon on the floor, and we will let you leave unmolested."

"Stand aside!" Surprised, he forgot to keep his eyes on his target.

Nect held a small device to the thug's arm, pressed a button, and the would-be kidnapper crumpled to the floor.

"Well done, everybody! Megra, call the principal. Andra, secure that weapon. You four, drag this oaf into the classroom. Segre and Thapi, go down and block the exit for his colleague. He's probably waiting in an unmarked vehicle with darkened glass. You'll have no trouble finding it. Darsenagre, get your jamming device onto the vehicle as soon as you can."

The youngsters leapt into action. Madhar withdrew to her office.

▭

jisporaVflacVmeblishVnrc

Greetings, Alliance Chair.

I have had a visit from a hired kidnapper.

Surveillance recordings of the attack upon my person will be included in tonight's *Science World* unless you immediately take steps to ensure my safety as I have requested.

I will soon have the attacker's vehicle stripped down and its origins ascertained. This information will also be broadcast unless I receive your full protection.

madharVnectVlatsinVux

The next hour was a busy one for Madhar and her students. Only the presence of a TV news crew persuaded the driver to abandon his vehicle. Once that was done, the electronics were stripped from it and taken to one of Madhar's labs. Government guards reported to the scientist: some took up positions throughout the institute, while others removed the still-unconscious kidnapper.

"Results?"

"Yes, professor," said Yura Gre, pushing back her glasses. "We can identify the codes and addresses."

"Who was it?"

"The Arpinata Chemical Company."

"Arpinata!" Madhar laughed coldly. "Well done. Say nothing to anyone else about this. Let me have your notes."

"Yes, professor."

She handed them over, smiling shyly.

"Full marks," said her teacher, smiling back.

Tella landed the flier on the strip midmorning. The tidal waters had swollen the rivers to their fullest, and Beauty was a pale semicircle high above their heads. Jim and his friend watched it as they stood next to the flier. No one came to greet them.

Jim walked first to the shed that Sopha had as good as demolished in his haste to escape. It had been rebuilt. No signs existed of the damage. Then he showed Tella the main building. All the doors were locked. There was no sign of life inside.

"Take me to the promontory," said Tella as Jim tried a door again.

"Oh...sure. Up this way."

It seemed to take Jim longer to reach the platform than before, even though the path was easier to follow than he remembered. The humidity, however, was no better.

Jim found the platform unchanged. He watched Tella circling with a frown of concentration on its pale brow, apparently fascinated by the markings carved into the rock.

"Jim!"

"What is it?"

"We must photograph this place from the flier. This is amazing. Quite amazing!"

"Sure, we can do that. Do you think you can decipher it?"

"Perhaps. I wonder if the Regdenir can."

"Well, I would guess they can. They built it."

Tella shook its head. "This is very ancient, perhaps older than the Barottin Regdenir. They may not know. I will ask, if we have the opportunity."

Jim stood, as he had before, on the westernmost end of the circular platform. He tried to recapture the wonder he had felt watching the planet rise. Beauty seemed pale and diminished in its half-dark phase, filtered through the sunlit air.

"It's strange," he said. "During their ceremony it all seemed so real and powerful. But now...It's like being in a theater the morning after a play. All the magic has gone."

Tella came to his side. "Do not underestimate the truth that can be conveyed in that way. The actors may have gone, but the insights you gained live with you. I do not doubt that you saw something beautiful, and that, if you had not been here with Sopha Luca, you would not have realized its importance."

Jim smiled and hung his head slightly. "Yeah, I guess you're right. It's a funny business."

Tella wandered away from him. Jim watched as the Neraffan squatted down beside some delicate carvings held in the sweep of a thicker line as it looped out from the center of the platform. Taking off a long glove, Tella pressed its forearm against the stone.

The lines and curves of the carving were echoed in the Neraffan's skin. Tella slowly moved its arm from side to side and watched the markings change. Jim could not see if the pattern was mimicked exactly or if it was only an echo of the original, but the look of intense concentration on Tella's face shone clearly.

"This is a wonderful place, Jim. These"—Tella swept its left arm out to encompass the whole platform—"are a treasure of enormous worth."

"If things go well here, perhaps they'll let you come back and study it."

"Ah, that would be an unlooked-for blessing."

Tella got up and nodded vigorously and replaced its glove. "Come, Jim. Let's see if our party has started without us!"

They made their way back to the retreat house as TMV began to set behind the mountains. Already the rivers were running less deep. The noises of birds and animals were again louder than the hissing and gurgling of the water.

There was still no sign of anyone at the retreat house. They boarded the flier, and Tella took it up to hover over the promontory, keeping one camera trained on the main building's doors. While Tella was absorbed in taking images of the carvings, Jim remembered they should check for messages.

$$\square\!\!=\!\!\square$$

g101VnectVlatsinVux

Greetings, Jim Able.

To emphasize my worries about your safety, I must tell you there was an incident here today. I am all right, thanks to the good discipline and courage of my students. However, I am, more than ever, concerned that your presence here will upset our political stability. No one has enough respect for our government to allow it to deal with you alone. There are many interested parties at work who are normally apolitical. In this case the boundaries overlap. You are a prize for the large corporations. You could become a board member of the finest companies on our world if you wished to. I would not recommend it, however.

I hope your meeting there will be without trouble. How do I contact your world if I do not hear back from you?

madharVnectVlatsinVux

---

madharVnectVlatsinVux

I am truly sorry that our being here is causing such problems. I had no idea things were so fragile. Perhaps we could meet alone with only the most senior politicians? I think it might be best to keep this in some way personal. What do you think?

Attached are instructions in case our mission fails. Thank you again, good friend.

g101VnectVlatsinVux

"Nothing from the Regdenir?" asked Tella.

"No," said Jim. "Maybe they're not coming?"

"I would be very surprised. It was settled that someone would come."

"Hmm. I guess you can take your time. We'll land again when you're done."

When the rivers were dry and both the planet and the sun had set, Jim and Tella walked out along the landing strip to look at the stars. Several of TMV's sister planets could be seen, fiercely bright against the background of the twinkling stars. Pointing to a fast-moving point of light crossing the sky over their heads, Tella wondered, "Is that a satellite or Sopha on patrol?"

"If you see the beginnings of a red glow, it's probably already too late," Jim deadpanned.

Tella laughed. "Ah, human humor. I love it."

Jim's eyes twinkled in the dark.

As they turned to walk back to the flier, the lights came on in the retreat house. In silence they walked up the landing strip and through the open doors.

There was no one in the fountain room, though the fountain had started to flow. Jim squatted down beside the water and let some wash over his hand. It was warm.

"They've only just arrived, I think," he said to Tella, who nodded silently.

They waited for several minutes before they heard noises coming from below them.

"There are rooms underground?" asked Tella.

"Apparently so. I had no idea."

Through the kitchen and the classroom, they heard footsteps approaching. Three blue-cloaked figures entered the fountain room and stood with wide eyes staring at the two aliens.

The three Regdenir said nothing but gestured to an area with seats at the end of the fountain room. Tella and Jim walked around the water and sat down. The Turcanians followed and sat in a row in front of them.

Tella began.

"I am Tella of Neraff. This is James Able of Earth. We greet you in the name of the people of Earth. We thank you for allowing this meeting."

The shorter of the Regdenir spoke first. He was old, and the bumps on his head seemed crusty. His eyes were flecked with white at the rims. His voice was deep and clear.

"I am Angara Myourn of the First Order. Welcome to our home. My friend and esteemed colleague is with us, Oorudi Coungow of the First Order. We have also asked Margrev Aplar of the Second Order to be a witness to all that is said and done here."

Margrev Aplar held a small recording device in his hand. "If our guests will permit, I shall use this device to ensure that nothing is missed."

Jim and Tella nodded.

Jim said, "Please do. Though it was allowing such a recording that caused much of the...difficulty of my previous visit."

Angara Myourn nodded and sighed. "We are aware of the various circumstances of what transpired here. We have many questions to ask you. I would like to address the matter of Sopha Luca, perhaps later in our conversation?"

"Okay."

"May we begin with a small question?" asked Tella. "We did not see you arrive. How did you come here?"

Angara Myourn frowned and then smiled. "It is a simple matter. The geography of this region, from the mountains to the ends of the marshes, is like our skeleton." He indicated his side. "The bones run parallel. The mountains run straight, and in between are the wetlands. There are many pathways under the mountains. We travel through where we can. This house lies at the end of many miles of underground paths. Pilgrims may come here for ceremonies and to study the Pongret M'dar, the stones of the promontory."

"They are beautiful and ancient," said Tella.

"Indeed so. They have stood there for at least a thousand years, if not more."

"They are not from the Regdenir, then?" asked Jim.

"No. Our ancestors placed them. For their sake we returned to the marshes, inhospitable though they are. We hold our ancestors in high regard."

"The carvings are well made to have lasted so long and still be clear to all," said Tella.

"We lack the skills to make such things in these late days. Their methods are lost. The carvings are a wonder for us."

"As must be their meaning?"

The Regdenir smiled and did not reply.

"Our first questions are of a more general nature," said Oorudi Coungow. "We see that your bodies are similar to ours, both in size and capacities. You can breathe our air, and our gravity must be similar to your own. How can this be? We see even in our own planetary system a great variety of conditions, which, we reason, should give rise to a variety of physiologies."

Tella replied, "That is correct. There are a vast number of different types of sentient beings. We tend to limit our dealings to those races similar to ourselves. We find trading with dissimilar races to be problematic. Your planet and these moons fall within the astronomical parameters that also produced our worlds."

The Regdenir nodded.

"How have you learned our language?"

Jim said, "From the audnir TV transmissions. From an analysis of what we saw and heard there, we learned enough to begin. I understand I have a Multoaf accent."

"Similar, but better educated, I think," replied Coungow with a smile.

"For interplanetary use, there is a new language called Standard. We will leave with you a training device and instructions for replication, if you wish to study Standard."

Angara Myourn spoke next. "You suggested in your messages that Beauty is to be found in other places. Do you know what we mean by Beauty?"

Jim and Tella looked at each other. Jim went first.

"I was...privileged to be present at a ceremony on the promontory above us when Beauty rose full into the night sky. Sopha Luca explained to me the place Beauty holds in your beliefs."

"The B'Goron Trahsa," Margrev Aplar said in confirmation.

Tella continued, "We understand from Sopha Luca's teaching that the presence of Beauty indicates for you that there is a place in the universe for those things all moral creatures desire: hope, love, and goodness."

Angara Myourn nodded. "It is well said."

Tella continued, "I have traveled much. I have lived on many worlds in my short life. I have listened to many wise people. Let me tell you of my own upbringing and the belief with which I was raised."

"Please."

"Our teachers say that, in the founding of the universe, three things were brought together: matter, energy, and 'Quavvour,' which is best translated as 'spirit.' We believe that beyond the confines of this universe of the three dimensions of space, and the fourth of time, there is an intelligence, about whom, because of our place within those dimensions, we can have no direct knowledge. To provide us with a link, an indirect experience of itself, the intelligence created Quavvour to surprise us and remind us whenever we meet it. The spirit is hidden in many places and in many people. It shines when we see it. It lifts us out of the dark. When found inside us and found in others, it inspires love. It is the root of our moral sense. This is our belief. I hear in your regard for Beauty an experience of Quavvour."

There was silence.

"Thank you, Tella of Neraff. And you, James Able of Earth, what of your beliefs?"

Jim suddenly felt an echo of his previous discomfort in this same room. He did not want to give a personal answer to the question. Tella had sounded like it really believed what it said. Jim didn't know where to begin; it was a long while since he had believed in anything.

"On Earth, there are a great variety of beliefs. Some hold that the question of a higher existence is unanswerable. Some believe in a multiplicity of higher beings who are in contact with us mortals. For some, the universe is a great cyclic event: a journey of constant improvement.

"Some believe, like Tella's people, that there is a single God, outside of our existence. My family...we believe this. We hold that, because of the limits on us and our experience, God has to bridge the Great Divide. We believe this was done by God's manifestation as an individual human, whose whole life was an expression of God's message. Direct experience of the unknowable became possible through Him. The message He brought was one of love." Jim paused. "This is the belief."

Again there was silence.

"How did your attendance at the B'Goron Trahsa touch your belief?"

Jim frowned. "It reminded me of it. Hearing Sopha Luca speak of the universe 'making sense,' of it being transformed, it seemed like he was saying something I was already familiar with."

Angara Myourn said again, "It is well said."

Margrev Aplar said quietly, "If I may contribute a question?"

Angara nodded.

"I hear behind your words a sadness, James Able. Can it be that you no longer follow your family's beliefs?"

Jim was shaken by the accuracy of the Regdenir's observation. He was silent for a moment.

"Not everyone believes to the same extent. I haven't had much time for belief for a long while. My parents' generation still attended regular services, but I do not. On Earth, such beliefs became much less influential when we first made contact with another world."

Angara Myourn frowned and said, "Please go on."

"I guess there is an element in our many beliefs that claims a 'special' place for our world: the idea that we have been chosen by God, for whatever purpose. How can that be squared with the existence of many other races, of other beliefs, multiplied again and again through the galaxies? It seems to diminish our world's importance somehow."

Tella's head was shaking. "For us, it did not. Our belief was already open to finding the revelation of Quavvour in many places, in the unexpected and the unknown. For us, that multiplicity deepens our belief."

Angara Myourn raised his hands and looked as if he would speak but, for a long while, nothing came. Then, reaching out to touch the sleeves of his fellow Regdenir, he said softly, "This is the matter that concerns us greatly: At the moment we saw a strange question appear in Regde99, from a stranger given access by Wehorulan Jiir"—he narrowed his eyes at Jim—"we knew only that this system was the sole repository of Beauty. We knew of nothing else." He turned his eyes to Tella and back to Jim. "That special revelation of which you speak was ours alone. Within such a short time, all of that has been challenged. How can we ever say to our people that Beauty is only one beauty among many? How can we face our children and tell them we were wrong?"

Tears appeared at the edges of Angara Myourn's eyes.

Tella spoke into the quiet, "You were not wrong. That Quavvour appears in many places, and in many ways, makes the universe *more* wonderful, not less. The joy and inspiration you gain from Beauty is multiplied, not divided."

"I stand on the first step of the flight to understanding this," said the old Regdenir. "There are many who will not go so far. It will take the greatest works of Margrev Aplar and his fellow poets and artists to change the hearts of a world."

Jim saw the pain in the expressions of his hosts. His own distance from the beliefs of his ancestors; his lack of connection, in fact, to so much of Earth's past, which grew from his life on a permanent station in an alien system; and the toll taken by constant traveling with the OEA all combined to leave him with only the dullest understanding of what they were going through. He could see the depth of their feeling, but he could not share it.

Jim recalled the old lady on the shuttle saying "It's so important to have roots, don't you think?" Now, Jim was caught between two contradictory conclusions: he was glad to be free of such potentially painful connections; he was envious of those who could care so much.

After a long and deep silence, Tella sat up and looked squarely at Myourn. "Let me say this to you, from the heart of my people. If you choose to travel to other worlds, come first to Neraff. Come to our spiritual leaders. They will welcome you as before-unknown cousins. There will be a feast of discussion and of doubts and of certainties. Come! Visit us."

"Thank you for your offer and for your goodwill. But it is much too soon to think of such things. If I may live long enough, perhaps I will see that day and sit at that feast."

Margrev Aplar took the old Turcanian's hand and said, "Perhaps it is time for refreshment?"

Myourn nodded, and they all stood.

Jim said, "We have some things in our flier that we would gladly share with you, if you wish."

Margrev Aplar replied, "It is well done. We will set a table here and share together."

CHAPTER ELEVEN

In the humid air of the forest Jim felt drained.

"Tella?"

"Yes, Jim?"

"How can you talk like that about your world? You said your kind...You're an abused minority, aren't you?"

"Yes. That is so. It is something that happens sometimes. When a religion becomes institutionalized, you might find individuals who can declare 'Quavvour may be found here, but Quavvour may not be found there.' As if, by saying so, they control what Quavvour will do. I try not to let that interfere with my own search. Quavvour will be there, at the right time, in the right place."

They set out their specially treated samples of food and drink along one end of the table. Jim recognized some of the food the Turcanians supplied, but not all. To his relief, there did not seem to be anything alive on any of the plates. The Regdenir seemed much more relaxed as they ate and drank.

While they were eating, Oorudi Coungow asked Jim, "Tell me of Madhar Nect. I understand she was the first you visited."

"She was—she is—a friend. She understands much about space travel already. But I'm concerned about her. She indicated she was in danger. I don't think the audnir are reacting well to exposure to an expanded galaxy. I think the business interests are flexing their muscles."

"That is not good. They behave so often like rodents in the sewer, running this way and that, biting each other's backs."

Jim raised an eyebrow at the tone in the Regdenir's voice but remembered that Sopha had been just as dismissive.

Coungow turned to Myourn. "Should we influence this struggle between the audnir? They will rearrange themselves into power blocks seeking affiliations with these new races."

He nodded. "We have a part to play. They do not deserve our help, but we can at least mitigate the worst of their excesses. See to it."

Coungow swept out of the room, leaving Jim and Tella wondering what was being set in motion by this brief, but ominous, conversation.

The other Regdenir went back to their chairs. Jim and Tella returned to their seats with long glasses of a milky drink, and the conversation resumed.

"It is time to talk of Sopha Luca," announced Myourn.

Jim and Tella waited politely.

"Every generation produces its own variety of offspring; some are dull, some are sharp, some are sharper than their parents ever were." The old face frowned while he thought. "And then there are those gifted in other ways: some are gifted in loyalty, in devotion, perhaps in passion for their faith. Sopha Luca is one such. His studies are his life. They are all to him. You know, I wonder that he has a family! Even now, he continues to contribute to every debate in Regde3. He has written some of the most excellent commentaries I have seen from his order." He looked a long while at Jim's face. "He will have told you about his studies, perhaps?"

"Yes, he showed me some of his contributions to the Regdekol. He told me about the audnir spacecraft and that you view what they did as sacrilegious."

Jim noticed a slight intake of breath in both the Regdenir. He could feel Tella become fully alert at his side.

"What else did he tell you?" asked Myourn.

"That was about it. He said you had been discussing whether the removal of the spacecraft was appropriate. He said he would soon bring the matter to a resolution."

"The spacecraft? The audnir spacecraft? He is going to remove it?"

"Yes, that's what he said."

The two Regdenir glanced at each other, and Myourn said, "Perhaps so."

Tella was on the hunt. "You feel there is something else he is engaged in?"

Myourn looked at Tella, his head slightly bowed. There was an awkward silence.

Tella spread his hands wide. "We must find him and prevent harm from being done. We need all the information you feel comfortable giving us."

Margrev Aplar shifted in his seat. "Perhaps if I did not record this part of our meeting."

"Agreed," said Myourn. Once the device was powered off, Myourn sat up straight. "Sopha Luca is his order's foremost scholar of the Maggnir. He has no interest in the spacecraft."

Jim's jaw dropped, and Tella turned to stare at him. "He never mentioned even their existence. I learned of them from Nect."

"Nonetheless, they are, and have been for some thirty years, his main obsession. Remember, you are audnir; he would not have told you everything."

Aplar took up the old Turcanian's words as Jim covered his face with his hands.

"This obsession of Sopha's, we now see as his being drunk on Beauty. Once we had heard of you and your search for Sopha Luca, we began to review his activities. We understood why he had obtained the scanning device. It was a profound piece of deduction —to go from his discovery of alien signals and interplanetary commerce to the realization that detecting small objects from great distances must be just one of many accomplishments of space travelers. He saw the potential for its use in his studies of the Maggnir. He would not dare to travel to Beauty, but he could observe it and its inhabitants from here. It was to be the crowning achievement of his life. He would contribute a vast body of observations about the Maggnir. But then we saw a change in his ambition."

Jim sighed. "He lied to me. He said the scanner was an afterthought. His main goal, he said, was to travel to Beauty to remove the relaunch module. I can't believe he took me in so easily." Jim inhaled deeply and swallowed. "I'm sorry. I talked with him, at that kitchen table, and corrected him on something he had misunderstood. He believed lasers were toys for children. I told him about their military uses. I put the idea in his mind."

Myourn continued, his voice thick with emotion, "We think he might have once stopped at observation. Regdekol threads have long shown his and others' belief that the Maggnir are not of Beauty. He wrote that they represent 'scars' on the face of Beauty, that Beauty had set a test for the faithful: to discover a way to heal these scars. He recently wrote that he had found a way. We believe he will use this audnir machine to eradicate the Maggnir."

Tella sat forward in its seat, its eyes darting across the floor. "Sopha can pinpoint any source of heat, such as forges or cooking fires—or people. He can sweep an entire area or pick off individuals one by one. Yes, what you say is possible, technically. But he is not a murderer, surely? Do you really think that one of your own could do this?"

The Regdenir did not answer.

Jim said quietly, "I think he could. He may have already started."

Tella frowned. "No, it is ridiculous. To destroy a whole population is bad enough, but to do it one by one?"

Jim shook his head and said, "It's just a matter of dedication, determination, and a lifetime's training in minutely detailed work. It takes the type of mind..."

There was a small silence as they looked at each other. Myourn said simply, "I ask for your help. You understand these devices. Perhaps, together, we may stop him."

Tella stood up. "Our thoughts are one. I can tell you more about the scanner and the laser. Jim, please see if Madhar Nect has been able to detect anything happening on Beauty."

Jim walked into the computer room. Several of the monitors had been removed. The one Sopha Luca had used to access the Deneb system was shut off. Jim sat in front of one of the live machines and sent Madhar a message.

---

madharVnectVlatsinVux

Greetings, Madhar Nect.

I hope your troubles are passing.

We have both good and bad news from the Regdenir. It is essential that we track Sopha Luca immediately.

Have you or your astronomers seen any activity on Mainworld? We need coordinates and times. This is truly urgent!

g101VnectVlatsinVux

---

g101VnectVlatsinVux

Greetings, Jim Able. I'm glad you remain alive and free.

I, too, am alive and, so far, free.

We have observed several strange things on Mainworld.

Southern Continent -coastal plain grid 5 -picture attached from midnight three days ago. This is the landing site.

Northern forests -grid 24, 25, and 26 -pictures attached from yesterday. Sorry the quality is not so good. I'll give this student low marks (it was I).

Last hour: an equatorial island -picture attached. Looks like a forest fire.

What are these vapor trails that are drifting across the pictures? Is this from his craft?

madharVnectVlatsinVux

---

g101VnectVlatsinVux

Greetings, Madhar.

Thanks for the information.

No, they are not from his craft. They are ozone columns from the interaction between the laser and the atmosphere.

We will stop him.

madharVnectVlatsinVux

Jim returned to the fountain room to find Tella pacing like an expectant father.

"Pilo told us. I did not take it seriously enough. He knew Sopha had multiple targets in mind. Come, we must go!"

"Go where?"

"To find him!"

"Look at these." Jim handed his friend the pictures transmitted by Nect.

"As we feared, he has started."

They took them over to the Regdenir.

Tella paced around them while Jim explained what they were looking at.

"How do we find him?" asked Myourn.

"I'm not sure," admitted Jim.

"We go to Beauty and find where he is operating!" Tella seemed incredulous that Jim had not said it himself.

"I don't think he's there."

"What?"

"Look at the damage to the atmosphere. That's going downwards, not coming up. He's not on Beauty. He's firing from here somewhere."

Tella was surprised and silent for a moment. "That doesn't make sense. Why wouldn't he go there?"

"He will not...physically touch Beauty himself," answered Myourn.

"That's right. As much as he can, Sopha will do it remotely." Jim held up his hand. "Let's get these to the flier and see if we can calculate a position from these times and locations."

"That won't be easy," warned Tella.

"What else do we have?"

Margrev Aplar stood and said, "You must do what you can. We cannot go with you. Tell us if there is something you would have us do."

Distracted by Tella's impatience, Jim tried to think. "How can we keep in contact? Do you have radios or something similar?"

"No, we do not use such things."

"What happens in an emergency? What if a pilgrim falls ill out here?" asked Tella.

"Ah, yes, there are emergency units, for use underground."

"Bring one. Let's see if it will work from orbit."

Tella calmed down during the analysis of the communications unit. Jim hoped he could connect it to the flier's comms array and have a reasonable chance of it working. They wrote down the call codes they should use and hurried out to the flier.

Jim launched himself into connecting the communicator while Tella began the search for the origin of the blasts hitting Beauty.

"This is James Able. Can you hear me?"

"Greetings, James Able, this is Margrev Aplar. I can hear you, though not well."

"Likewise, Margrev Aplar. This is as good as I can make it. It should be enough. You should also be able to call us if you need to."

"It is well done, but now we will wait to hear of your progress."

"Okay."

Jim went to Tella. "How are we doing?"

"I'm not at all sure. These calculations must be wrong. Why would he be hanging out in space?"

"Why not? He doesn't want his own flier to cast a shadow. It makes sense that he'd move off to one side or the other."

"I suppose so."

Tella stopped and looked at Jim. "TMV-Two."

"Okay. I see."

They rolled the flier down the strip for an easy takeoff. The Regdenir stood in the doorway of the retreat house, watching the black shape rise into the pale eastern sky.

While they climbed into orbit, Tella turned to his colleague. "Jim?"

"Tella."

"I should warn you about something."

"You're going to tell me you've been instructed to blow Sopha to pieces if he resists."

"No, not Sopha, just the laser. I don't have to bring it back."

"Understood. I don't know how we're going to do this."

"Nor do I."

"TMV-Two has only a residual atmosphere. Sopha won't be able to leave his flier."

"Are you sure?"

"No...I don't know. We don't know what Turcanian physiology can do. You're right."

The flier reached orbit, and they surveyed the scene before them. Glinting anonymously in both the Turcanian sun and the reflected green glow cast by Beauty itself was TMV-II. Its surface was brown and cratered. They could see no activity.

"I don't see him," said Jim.

"We only know that's where he was. He may not be staying in one place," replied Tella.

They were both poring over their scanner displays in the navigation suite. TMV-II and its craters were slowly passing below them.

"Let's do one more pass. Then we'll start a wide search." Jim sighed and ran his fingers through his hair.

"Agreed."

Tella made the flier rise slightly and pointed the nose toward the Turcanian moon once more, gently moving the craft against its spin. Jim set the scanners once more to record anything that wasn't rock.

Tella returned from the cockpit to join Jim at the scanners. As they moved into the moon's shadow, the craft rocked slightly.

"What was that?" asked Jim.

"I have no idea," said Tella, a puzzled expression settling as deeply as it could on the round face.

The craft rocked again. An alarm sounded in the cockpit. They leapt to their feet and rushed through the narrow doorway.

"The blast shields have tripped!" called Tella over the noise of the alarm.

"Did we hit something?" asked Jim.

"Unknown."

"I'll set up the wide sweep."

Jim threw himself back into the navigation suite and set the scanners for a spherical sweep of their immediate vicinity.

"Nothing large showing nearby!" he shouted to Tella. "We have enlarging areas of hot micro-debris off the port wing—six hundred feet and three hundred fifty feet."

Tella swung the craft round to point at the area.

"What's this?" Jim pointed to a streak growing from the edge of the scanning area.

"Incoming weapons fire?"

They looked at each other in surprise. The craft rocked violently as the missile exploded.

JIM ABLE OFFWORLD

A'NIR

4

ED CHARLTON

AUTHOR OF "THE ALERONDE TRILOGY"

CHAPTER TWELVE

Tella was already back in the cockpit, and the flier was dipping into the atmosphere of TMV-II, before Jim had truly comprehended what was happening. He switched the scanner to view farther toward the origin of the hostile fire.

"One contact. Profile suggests a PR233, solo flier. Weapons firing!" Jim reported.

"Avoiding."

Their flier lurched farther into the atmosphere and banked hard. Jim saw the missile explode, but Tella had moved them clear enough not to feel the blast.

"This is not good, Jim."

"Agreed. It seems he's been shopping at other places besides Pilo's House of Lasers."

"Without knowing what he's got, I'm loath to get in front of him again."

"Let's try talking first."

"Agreed."

Jim activated the standard ship-to-ship system.

"Sopha Luca. Sopha Luca. Reply, please. This is James Able. Reply, please."

There was no reply. As Jim began to transmit again, another missile entered the atmosphere ahead of the flier.

"Unbelievable!" cried Tella. "He knows where we are, and he's even compensating for the minimal refraction of the atmosphere! Jim, he is good at this!"

"Yeah, great. If you're so impressed with him, I'll have him stuffed and mounted for you."

"Hah! Let's see what we can do here."

Tella looped the flier back up to the edge of the atmosphere and threw the craft around the smaller moon, its engines howling with the sudden strain.

"If I'm correct, we should have just blindsided him."

"How?"

"I think he's using his scanner array on TMV-One to follow us. Around here, we should be eclipsed by TMV-Two. He'll have to come and find us himself."

"What if he doesn't?"

"We have time to see if he's done us any damage."

"And he'll be able to carry on with his new hobby while we do."

"Keep on the scanners and power up the weapons modules. I'll check on our skin."

Jim did not need the instructions. He opened the safety catches on the weapons controls and sat poised to act should Sopha's flier come around the moon. Tella opened the maintenance stores and took out a small camera unit. He unhooked the door of a small clear hatch in the ceiling and loaded it inside. He restored the seals and returned to the cockpit.

"Okay. Launching remote eye. Let's see how close he got."

Tella watched the monitor receiving the images from the camera. The flier's black wings rolled by, small glowing spots showing where missile fragments had melted into the enamel coating.

"Nothing too bad. No pressure leaks. Nothing broken off."

"How did he track us so easily? This is supposed to be unde-tectable!"

"My fault," admitted Tella. "We haven't been running quietly. He had clues to follow. I'm putting that right."

"Good. Being fried isn't in my contract."

Within a few minutes Tella announced, "Running silently. He can't find us."

"Thank you. Now what?"

"We can wait, or we can try to find him. You're the expert. What do you think Sopha will do next?"

Jim sat with his head in his hands. He stood to pace the confines of the flier. He unpacked Liz Curacao's paper folder. He sat again in thought.

"Tella?"

"Jim."

"Check my math here. To get accuracy to one or two meters, how far apart do the first and the last scanning nodes need to be?"

Tella leaned down to look at the scrawl of figures that Jim had written on the back of one of the sheets of paper. Curls and strokes echoed up its finger as it traced the flow of the calculations.

It nodded. "Yes. That is correct."

"The spread is too big. He can't fit them both on TMV-One."

"Hmm. Interesting."

They were both silent for a moment.

"That's why he was on TMV-Two," said Tella.

Jim shook his head. "We didn't see any sign of a node. If it were there, we would have seen something."

"But he needs the spread, so it has to be!"

"How can he hide it?"

"There's no way...except we know he purchased other armaments. Could he also have gotten some concealment technology?"

"If he did, we're sunk. Without knowing where he bought it or who it's from, we can't know what kind of system it is or even begin to think of countermeasures." Jim threw down his pen. "Damn him!"

He felt again the rising desire to be gone from the area. Turcanis

Major was no longer where he wanted to be. It could sort itself out for all he cared. Tella was watching him closely.

"Jim. You must think clearly."

Tella sat down opposite Jim.

"I have been around humans for several years now. I know they are wonderful creatures in many ways. But you all share one major problem."

Jim bit back his irritation at Tella.

The Neraffan continued, "You do not manage your resources well."

Jim frowned.

"You try to use the same resources over and over in a variety of tasks. You do not specialize well. How often, Jim, have you pried something open with the blade of a screwdriver, or hammered a nail with the side of your pliers?"

Jim laughed. "What are you on about?"

"You, Jim. Since Ch'Garratt, you have not known if you are screwdriver or hammer. Your boss, the troubled Elizabeth Curacao, also does not know her place. I do not understand why this is so difficult for you humans."

Jim turned away but glanced sideways at the Neraffan, unwilling to continue the conversation but curious enough to listen.

"You blame yourself for a lapse of judgment on Ch'Garratt, for failing to notice something important."

"I've never told you about that."

"During the latter part of the night we got drunk, you talked of nothing else."

"Oh."

"It is obvious to any nonhuman that your skills are of a different type. If Elizabeth Curacao had wanted someone who could count the eyelashes on all the faces in a crowd, she would have found one. You, Jim, have a different set of abilities. You have empathy for alien races. You can work your way into their technology and into their minds. You astonish me with the technical feats you have performed here. Your ease with me is something I treasure."

Jim waved his hand in embarrassment.

"You have met Sopha. You understood the fire of his belief. We do not need to count eyelashes, Jim. We need to use the understanding you already have. I'll ask again: what will he do next? You are the only one in the universe in a position to answer. You are the correct resource for this job. We have no other; we have none better."

Jim stared at Tella for several seconds. "Bastard."

Tella frowned and cocked its head to one side.

Jim continued, breaking into a small smile, "I'm never going to let you get me drunk again."

Then, Jim thought for a while in silence.

"Let's go back into orbit around TMV-One. I want to hear what the Regdenir have on Sopha right now."

"Yes, Jim," agreed Tella, smiling.

Jim called Aplar. "Greetings, Margrev Aplar."

"Greetings, James Able. Have you located Sopha Luca?"

"We have encountered him, but we do not know where he is now."

"Ah, that is unfortunate."

"What do you know of his movements there?"

"We know he is currently contributing to the Regdekol. It is the first time today that he has been active."

"Yes, he was...distracted earlier."

Tella offered a question. "Is there anything in his latest contributions to indicate his current state of mind, or perhaps his immediate intentions?"

"I do not know. We would have to spend more time in analysis."

"Please do. We need as much information as you can pass to us."

"Agreed."

Jim ended the call. "Okay, we know he's still linked in. Myourn said he had friends who shared his conclusions about the Maggnir. I presume they're at least giving him moral support."

"A strange expression, under the circumstances."

"I guess so. The only opposition he knows about is us—or more specifically, me."

"And he has prepared himself for this eventuality."

"We need to do something—something that he will not expect, something that will get him back down to the surface, where the Regdenir can get hold of him."

"We could damage his craft sufficiently to necessitate a landing," offered Tella.

"Risky, but an option. I was hoping for something more...personal."

Tella thought for a moment. "We could kidnap his family."

Jim's eyes widened in shock. "That's not quite what I had in mind. But...No, it wouldn't work, would it?"

"Why not?"

"He loves Beauty above all things. Which would win if we made him choose between his family and his mission?"

Tella nodded. They were silent, staring at each other.

"All we need is to get his flier where I can get on board," said Tella. "Nothing else matters. Once on board, I can destroy the laser. End of story."

"Agreed. So let's look at it again. Three options: one, he lands on TMV; two, he lands on TMV-One; three, he lands on TMV-Two."

"Okay. TMV is difficult. He doesn't want to land there, nor do the other Regdenir."

"TMV-One is difficult. He doesn't want to be stopped. He'll stay up until he's finished now," Jim said.

"TMV-Two. We know he goes there. He was waiting for us there."

"But we don't know for sure that he lands on it. We think he has the last scanning node there..."

They both stopped, openmouthed.

"The scanning nodes!" Jim exclaimed, "Are we idiots or what?"

"Call Aplar."

"Margrev Aplar? This is James Able."

"Greetings, James Able. Sopha Luca is not currently active in the Regdekol. Is he, as you put it, 'distracted' again?"

"Ah...Not that we know. Listen, we need you to find out where he has put the scanning devices around your moon. I remember Dlavi Heruc admitted that one of them was on the roof of his home. We must find the others."

"This will not be easy without Sopha Luca's knowing what we do."

"I don't think that matters."

"Wait," said Tella. "We don't need them all—just one. If we know the frequency he is using, we can blind him."

Jim nodded.

"Okay, Margrev. Go to Heruc's house and call us from there. We need information from the control panel of the device."

"Very well. I shall call you immediately after we arrive."

"Now," began Jim, turning to Tella. "How do we jam the signal such that he has to land somewhere?"

"Hmm. He has to be able to trace it, but not stop it remotely."

Jim smiled. "Nect!"

"Is there somewhere we can land near her?"

"I'm sure."

---

madharVnectVlatsinVux

Greetings, Madhar Nect.

We have a plan to stop Sopha Luca.

We need you to arrange a transmission on a particular frequency.

We need to land somewhere near the site of the transmission.

We will use it to lure Sopha to land as well.

Can you do this?

Where?

g101VnectVlatsinVux

---

g101VnectVlatsinVux

Greetings, Jim Able.

You don't do things simply, do you? Why can't you shoot his engines and leave him to drift in space?

The Institute has a TV relay tower. We can patch something in there. There is a sports field below the tower. It should be good to land on.

When will you arrive? I have to get authorization for this. That will not be easy, particularly in the present climate.

Attached is a map.

madharVnectVlatsinVux

---

madharVnectVlatsinVux

Greetings, Madhar Nect.

We are on our way. Forget the authorization. Let's plan to apologize after, rather than ask before. We'll help clear up the paperwork after we're done.

Just make sure no games are being played on the field.

g101VnectVlatsinVux

---

g101VnectVlatsinVux

Greetings, Jim Able.

I'm going to regret this, aren't I?

If there is to be violence, I must make sure the students are all evacuated.

madharVnectVlatsinVux

---

madharVnectVlatsinVux

Greetings, Madhar Nect.

We hope there will be no violence. Our hope is simply to gain access to Sopha's craft.

That should be enough for our purposes.

Relax. Nothing can go wrong.

g101VnectVlatsinVux

CHAPTER THIRTEEN

It was early morning at the Latsin Institute when the jet-black shape of the flier descended from the clear air. Several students stopped jogging around the perimeter of the sports area to stand wide-eyed and openmouthed.

Madhar Nect approached, driving a small open-top vehicle. Several of her students were standing in the back, holding on to the rollover bar. Four more hung on to the back and sides. As he walked down the entrance ramp, Jim heard their shouting and saw them pointing.

"So much for doing this quietly," he muttered to Tella.

"You are already a TV celebrity."

"I guess so."

Madhar brought the vehicle to a sudden halt in front of the flier. Her passengers leapt away and began to run around and under its wings, calling excitedly to each other.

"Jim Able. You are traveling in style this time!" said Madhar Nect. To her students she called, "Take plenty of pictures. I want every child to own the model of this one too."

She and Jim shook hands, and the Turcanian drew the human into a hug.

"Oof! Madhar, this is Tella of Neraff."

They turned to greet the Neraffan.

"Madhar Nect, I am happy to meet with you," said Tella, holding out a gloved hand.

"Tella of Neraff. I..."

Madhar stopped, her hand half-raised, as she stared at Tella's face.

"What's the matter?" asked Jim.

"I'm sorry...You seem...Your skin...Do you change color?"

Tella smiled. "That depends."

"Oh my! You're a gallassid! I had never imagined!"

"What do you mean, 'gallassid'?" asked Jim, feeling that the name meant nothing good.

"I'm sorry; I don't mean to be rude. We have folktales of creatures who are like glass. They have no color or features of their own. I had never imagined that there was any truth to such tales."

Jim turned to Tella. "Have your people been here before?"

"I have not heard of it."

Madhar stepped forward, took Tella's hand, and shook it.

"Please forgive me. I hope I haven't caused offense. They are old tales..." She hesitated and then continued quietly, so that her students would not overhear, "They are superstitious tales. The gallassidnir are rarely the good guys, if you understand me. You may find a certain...caution in peoples' reactions to you."

"I understand. In fact, I would prefer to have little contact with your people for now. I have a mission to complete. We can turn our minds to cultural anthropology and more social matters when Jim and I have accomplished our task."

"Okay. Let's get to work. I'll take you to the tower. Do you have the frequency?"

Jim and Tella walked with her, followed by the group of chattering students.

"Margrev Aplar relayed to us the frequency setting from one of Sopha's scanners," Jim told Madhar. "We need to send a disrupting signal at this frequency. It should be something he can easily trace to here. Enough to make him land to investigate."

"He'll see your craft. He'll know it's a trap."

"We'll take care of that," said Jim, smiling. "This one is a whole lot more sophisticated than the last thing I came in."

The room at the base of the TV relay tower was small. Jim, Tella, Nect, and three students were more than it could comfortably hold.

One of the students took the details of the frequency from Jim.

"Professor?"

"Yes, Glav?"

"What are we going to transmit? If it isn't a TV or a radio that's receiving it, he won't get any idea of the message."

"Don't worry. He'll work it out. Patch in the call signal from the campus radio."

There was general amusement at this instruction.

"What are you sending?" asked Tella.

"It's just a repeated sequence of letters identifying the Institute's radio station. The authorities require a particular identification format."

She paused to smile. "They have us sending out 'LIRS' for 'Latsin Institute Radio Station.' This lot"—she gestured to the students—"think it's funny."

At Tella's puzzled expression, Madhar continued, "'Lirs' is the slang name for a sexually transmitted disease."

"Ah, I see," said Tella, shaking its head.

There were a few minutes of quiet concentration.

"Transmitting now, Professor. Power at the highest mark."

"Thank you. Jim, how long before he notices?"

"Immediately," Jim replied. "It may take him a moment or two to track down the signal."

"In that time, we must prepare for his arrival," said Tella.

"Okay, then, what do we do?" asked Madhar.

"Please have your students move to a place of safety."

"Okay, you three! Outside!"

There was a general groan of disappointment.

"Come on, we have to let our visitors do their work. We can buy them a drink in the bar afterward."

"Really? Do you drink alcohol?" Glav blurted out.

Jim smiled, glanced at Tella, and said, "Only in moderation."

Happy with the prospect of a further meeting with the aliens, they rejoined their fellows outside. Nect gestured to one of them to drive the vehicle away from the tower.

"I'll stay and make sure this works."

She grabbed a student by the arm and whispered in her ear, "Make sure the security cameras get everything that happens!"

The student glanced up at the tower, nodded, and climbed aboard.

Tella waited until they were safely away before using the remote control unit to close the flier and have it launch itself into orbit once more.

"I hope we get it back," muttered Jim.

"If I may quote a good friend of mine, 'Relax. Nothing can go wrong.'"

"Bastard," Jim said with a smile.

They stood side by side, watching the shadow diminish to a black dot and vanish.

"So, Madhar, when do I meet your government?" asked Jim.

"Huh. Didn't your Regdenir friends tell you?"

"What?"

"They are flexing their muscles again. For the first time in a hundred years, they're holding the threat of power disruptions over our heads."

"Really?"

"What demands are they making?" asked Tella.

"Oh, I don't know—some sort of joint meeting with their big chiefs and the inner circle of the government. It's playing as a sort of power grab while we're suffering a little instability. They don't want you meeting us without their guys being there."

Jim laughed and said, "It depends on your point of view, doesn't it?"

"It does?"

"Sure. Doesn't it seem reasonable that, faced with contact with other worlds, you might present a joint response? You know...all the people of your world?"

"Well," she smiled, "we'd expect them to climb at least partway down from their trees."

Tella said, "If I understand the metaphor correctly, they have already begun to do that. But I think your people will have to begin to take a broader view also."

The scientist nodded. "That's not going to be simple."

"It never is, but world by world, it happens. It is a path that you have to walk. You begin; you end. It is what it is."

She nodded again and was silent. A small alarm sounded in Jim's pocket. He took out a small black box.

Tella asked, "He is here already?"

"His flier is in proximity to ours."

"That was too quick."

"Will he see your craft? Is it in danger?" asked Nect.

"No," Tella said, "he will not know it is there."

"Neat trick." Her eyes flashed at Jim.

"No, Madhar, you can't buy it. Not yet."

They laughed but soon became serious again.

"What's next?" asked Madhar.

"In case he is already onto us, I must prepare," said Tella solemnly. He handed the flier's remote control to Jim without comment.

"Okay," said Jim.

"What's Tella going to do?" Nect asked Jim as Tella moved back into the control room.

"Take off its clothes."

"Really? Oh. I see."

"Or rather you don't see. Hopefully, neither will Sopha Luca."

"Another extremely neat trick."

As they waited for Tella to come back out, Madhar Nect asked a question that had been troubling her.

"Jim, is Tella male or female?"

Jim raised his eyebrows and smiled at his friend.

"Remember never to ask Tella that question. Tell your students they may not ask it either; it causes great offense."

Madhar buzzed to herself. "How about that." She shook her head. "There's so much to learn. I guess there'll be weirder things ahead of us than that."

"Too true."

They looked around at the control building. Jim went inside and saw Tella's robe, boots, and gloves tidied away under a desk.

"Tella?"

There was no answer.

Jim went back into the bright morning air and stood shoulder to shoulder with his Turcanian friend.

Jim and Madhar waited for more than half an hour. Birds flocked in the middle of the games field, rising suddenly and then quickly descending to resume feeding in the grass. The distant sounds of the Institute drifted over on the slight breeze.

"It looks like you managed to get everyone away from here."

"Only this area. I said I was setting off a test rocket," replied Nect.

"I guess they believed you."

"Oh yes, they expect the unexpected from me. That's the secret of my success. I had more trouble persuading my new bodyguards that they didn't need to come after me this morning. I sent them off to guard my best students instead."

"The price of fame?"

"It's all your fault."

"I guess so."

"Don't think I'm not grateful. Whatever happens here, I'm glad to have lived to see these days—my world knowing it's not alone."

A black speck appeared in the distance. It traveled overhead.

"What do you think?" asked Nect.

"That's him. He's checking out the area. Let's get a little way inside."

They stood in the doorway of the control building, craning their necks to see the flier return.

The noise of its engines came first. It slowly moved down over the field from behind the tower.

To Jim's dismay, Sopha did not land but set the flier to hover twenty feet above the grass. The craft turned to point its nose and weapons at the doorway.

"Madhar Nect! This is Sopha Luca of the Third Order. Come out into the open where I can see you!" The Regdenir's voice boomed across the open field.

"Oh shit," said Jim quietly.

"He doesn't know it's you," said Nect. "I'll go out and see what happens."

"Be careful. He's got the scent of blood in his nose."

"So do I." Madhar inhaled sharply, drew back her shoulders, and walked out into the open before the menacing craft.

Jim stayed in the shadows, looking closely at the alterations Sopha had made to his flier. The missile battery was an old-fashioned design, requiring a landing to restock. Jim could see five missiles remaining to be fired. More worrying was the laser cannon hung below the cockpit of the flier. It looked like a thoroughly professional job. Sopha must have read the instructions very carefully. It was attached to the hull with two neat lines of spring-loaded grips. All the cabling was out of sight, as per regulations.

Madhar shouted in the direction of the flier. "Sopha Luca of the Third Order, greetings and welcome to the Latsin Institute. You are welcome to land."

"Madhar Nect, you will cease the transmission of your call sign."

"I don't know what you mean. I am not familiar with the equipment in here. If there is a problem, perhaps you can help me resolve it? I understand your knowledge of technology is as great as, if not greater than, mine."

Jim muttered under his breath, "Nice one. Keep it up."

"You lie! Cease the transmission, or I will destroy this facility!"

"No! You can't risk starting trouble like that. We can sort out this problem, I'm sure. Just come down and talk."

"You are audnir; there can be no talk between us. Stand aside or be destroyed!"

"Wait! There's someone..."

She turned in panic toward Jim.

"I'll come out," Jim called.

He walked toward the scientist, his arms in the air in what he hoped the Turcanian would realize was a gesture of surrender.

"Sopha Luca!" he called. "Don't do this. Your own people are saying you have to stop what you are doing to Beauty!"

"James Able. You should not have returned. You have lied to all you have met. I will not let you defile my world any longer."

Jim's eyes flashed to the mechanisms under the wings of the flier. He saw a missile drop from its protected cradle into the firing clamps. At the same time, he saw something move under the center of the craft. A grip had sprung open at one side of the laser. The next grip popped open. Jim realized that Sopha had allowed the flier to drift closer to the ground. It was now only about ten feet above the field, low enough for Tella to clamber up onto the laser cannon.

That Tella was in action was little immediate help to Madhar and Jim, face-to-face with an armed missile.

Suddenly, the sound of gunfire froze the moment. Halfway down the field, two fast-moving vehicles were racing along the track. Madhar's bodyguards were shooting into the air.

The combination of Tella's courage and initial success and the arrival of help from the guards gave Jim a brief hope of victory. He grabbed the scientist's arm and pushed her into a run across the face of the control building. There was a hiss from the flier as the missile launched. The control building erupted in a ball of orange fire. Jim and Madhar were thrown head over heels across the grass.

Jim scrambled to his feet and dragged the Turcanian up into a staggering run. Debris was raining down on them as they tried to close the distance between themselves and the approaching vehicles.

Behind them, Sopha turned his flier and pressed the engines

into high gear. The TV tower was crumbling into its own base. The transmission had ceased. He was free to return to his sacred mission. As he turned over the games field, the flier was rising steadily.

The flock of birds had panicked at the explosion and the sudden motion of the black craft.

For every landing on his landing strip, Sopha Luca had followed the correct procedure; he was meticulous in doing so. But this time, he had not intended to land. This time, he had not closed the intakes for the heat exchangers when he entered the atmosphere. In his haste and anger, he had not done as the flier's instruction manual had told him he always must.

The birds swarmed up in a cloud of wings and distressed cries only to be sucked hard into the intakes. The first Sopha knew of his mistake was the sound of small explosions from inside the flier's outstretched wings as several birds were incinerated.

The flier's nose dipped suddenly and plowed into the ground of the athletics track beside the games field. The remaining missiles, ripped open by the impact, detonated with a muffled rumble. The automatic ejection system fired the pilot into the air. When the cockpit module hit its apogee, the parachute opened immediately.

A sudden silence fell over the games field. The bodyguards had piled Madhar into a vehicle and surrounded her. They were looking askance at Jim, in awe at the grounded flier, and incredulously at the burning TV tower. They waited for the scientist to give them instructions.

Jim was shouting, "Tella! Tella! Are you there?"

Madhar swung around to Jim. "Where is it? Where's the gallassid?"

"Under the flier! Tella had gotten up onto the underside of it."

"Then it may still be there..."

The scientist looked in horror at the smoking wreck.

"We have to find Tella. If it fell, it may be unconscious...hurt..."

"Find it? You can't see it!"

Jim shook his head, his ears still ringing from the blast.

"Get a line of people out here, shoulder to shoulder. From where it was hovering...across...to there." He pointed at the growing pall of smoke.

"Finding people won't be a problem."

A huge crowd of students and faculty was running toward them and toward the flier.

Madhar pointed at the supervisor of her guards. "You! Get them organized. They're to search the ground from here, right across the field. Pick up every piece of debris. Call if they find a gallassid."

"A what?"

Madhar took her fellow Turcanian's arm and led him a step away from Jim. "You think a gallassid any stranger than that?"

The guard was silent a moment, looking from her to Jim and back.

"Yes, ma'am. We'll call with whatever we find."

"And I want you, *personally*, to secure the Regdenir from the flier."

"That was a Regdenir? I thought it was another...alien."

"You'll soon see. Make sure he doesn't get away."

"At once, ma'am."

Jim walked slowly behind the line of students. Occasionally one would stoop and pick up a bit of debris from the explosion. The nearer they got to the edge of the field, the sicker he felt. Already he was blaming himself for not keeping Sopha talking longer. Tella had only needed a few more seconds—perhaps. A few more seconds that might have meant the difference between a life continued and a life curtailed.

Suddenly the line broke. A female student had screamed. Jim was there in an instant. There was something green and grasslike that was obviously not grass.

"Tella! Can you hear me?"

Jim was kneeling, trying to work out which way Tella was lying. He ripped off his shirt and laid it over the body. The gray color washed over Tella's limbs. A student fainted.

The vehicle arrived with Nect and a bodyguard.

"Put it in the back!" instructed Madhar.

Jim took the feet and the guard, the shoulders. Tella groaned as they picked it up and, again, as they slid it onto the seat.

"It's okay, fella. You're okay now."

Madhar grabbed Jim's arm.

"I hope you can help Tella. We don't have the medical skill to deal with something like this!"

"No...Nor do I. At least we have to get it somewhere warm and comfortable. We'll take it step by step from there."

"Medical room!" she called.

Jim climbed into the vehicle beside Tella.

They loaded their patient onto a bed in the medical room, Tella's body turning as white as the surrounding sheets.

"It looks like he's cut there," said a nurse to Jim, pointing at Tella's shoulder.

"I guess so." Jim didn't think it was the time to correct Tella's gender."

"I'll keep an eye on him."

"Thank you. And thank you for being so...accepting of us."

The nurse smiled and said, "We all watch Professor Nect's show. I'm really glad to get a close look at you."

Jim nodded and went out into the air. He looked up and remembered the flier. He felt instinctively for the control unit. His pocket was empty.

"Oh shit!"

CHAPTER FOURTEEN

He looked around for Madhar. She was nowhere to be seen. A gaggle of students was standing in the corridor to the medical room. Jim saw two of the three who had been with him in the tower control room.

"Hey! You guys, I need your help."

The two moved forward, their friends watching wide-eyed.

"In the control room we had a device—a remote unit for our flier. You may have seen us using it."

One of them nodded.

"It may still be in there or nearby. We have to find it! Do you understand?"

They nodded and followed him through the door.

"I am Jim Able, by the way."

"Yes, sir, we know. We saw you on TV. I am Frett Amtir," said the boy.

"My name is Rowa Culan," said the girl, her eyes sparkling under her brows.

By the time Jim and the students found a vehicle and had driven it back to the remains of the TV tower, the fire-fighting crew was in place and busy.

The open remains of the control room were awash in fire-retar-dant foam. Jim stood, shaking his head in despair.

"Are you sure it was in there, sir?"

Jim sighed. "I think so." He looked around. "Let's try and search the ground this way. I think that's where I ran when this went up. We may be lucky."

Jim had not anticipated the effect of TV stardom. Within a few minutes, his number of helpers had grown to twenty.

A whoop went up from a couple of young girls. Clutching the control unit, they rushed over to Jim. The whole group gathered around him, peppering him with questions as he checked for damage. He considered bringing the flier back immediately but looked around at the expectant faces, the scene of devastation around the destroyed tower, and the groups of officials crisscrossing the games field.

"I'll bring my flier back down a bit later," he announced to his young fans.

There was a mumble of disappointment.

"We'd better check up on my partner."

Some climbed into the vehicle; the rest jogged along on either side.

While they traveled, one asked, "Is your friend really a gallassid?"

"I don't think so, not as you know it. I suppose your legends might be based on some encounter with a Neraffan, but I doubt we can ever truly know."

"What's a Neraffan?"

"That's what Tella is. Its world is called Neraff."

"Is it far away?"

"Yes, it is. Much farther than my world."

"Will more of you come from your world?"

"Oh, I don't know. If your government invites us, yes, but not otherwise."

"Who was in the ship that crashed?"

"I can't tell you that. That's a matter for the authorities."

"I think it was another alien," said a voice from one side.

"Well...No, I can't say. I'm sorry."

By the time they reached the medical room again, Jim's temper was getting short from having to repeat the same line over and over.

Jim was waiting with Tella and hoping it would recover consciousness long enough to describe its injuries. Madhar, flanked by two bodyguards, rushed into the room.

"Jim, we have a small problem."

"What's up?"

"The word is out about your presence here. Also spreading abroad is the notion that there is an alien craft lying in a field, ripe for stripping down and reverse engineering. I know of three companies dispatching teams to clear it away for us. If they arrive together, they'll fight over it."

"Uh-oh."

"Any ideas?"

"Get everyone away from the flier. Is there anything we need from it?"

"Like what?"

"Like evidence against Sopha Luca?"

The scientist shook her head. "Don't worry about that. He's their responsibility. You might want to check in with them, but..."

"Where is he, by the way?"

"Who?"

"Sopha Luca!"

"I...I told Burat to go and get him! Where is the idiot?" She turned to one of her guards. "Find your boss and report back to me. He was supposed to be collecting the pilot of that flier."

"Yes, ma'am."

"So," said Jim, "I'd better bring back the flier."

With a glance at Tella's white face, he went outside to use the remote. He called the flier and worried that it might not be easy to clear everyone away from the field.

The sight of the sleek black craft coming in slowly over the Institute had an energizing effect. There was sufficient doubt abroad as to the intentions of the aliens that the field cleared quickly. He walked halfway toward the craft as it settled on the grass. He turned to see Madhar driving after him.

"Jim!"

"Hi, what's up?"

"I just wanted to make sure I had a look inside this one!"

"Come on board."

He led the Turcanian up the ramp and closed the door.

Madhar looked around in amazement.

"Take a seat," Jim said, pointing at the copilot's seat. "Don't touch anything."

"No problem. What does this do?" She pointed at a control panel in front of her.

"I'll explain it all later. We have a job to do."

The flier lifted gently into the air. Jim turned it slowly and took up position near Sopha's downed craft. He opened the baffles on the weapons units, targeted the wreck, and checked once more for signs of life.

"There's a column of vehicles approaching the wreck," he said to Madhar.

"Can I see them?"

"There." Jim pointed to a small monitor screen.

"I can't tell who it is. Shoot now. Don't let them get any closer."

Jim fired. He carved the flier into small pieces. The paths of his beams left deep troughs in the bodywork that were edged with glowing orange worms of metal and ceramic. He made three passes over the wreckage to ensure nothing large was left intact. Finally, he fired two high-explosive charges into the heap of burning chunks.

"Okay," said Jim. "Good enough. I think it's safe."

He felt a grim satisfaction that he had completed Tella's mission —by destroying the laser with the rest of the craft.

"Thank you," said Madhar. "I wouldn't like to see our world become a technological serfdom. You've never seen our businessmen in operation, have you? You just did us all a big favor."

"I'd like to get back to Tella now."

"I'm sorry. Of course, you must."

"But, you know, while we're here..."

Jim pointed the flier to the sky and took the scientist for her first real view of her home.

Madhar Nect was silent as she walked down the ramp from the flier. She had dried the tears from her eyes.

"If that column of trucks is anything to go by, I'm going to need a guard," said Jim.

"You're right." Madhar stopped at the foot of the ramp. "Stay right here, Jim. I'll bring Tella. You two should go back into orbit until we see how this turns out."

"Are you sure?"

"It'll be best."

"Okay."

Madhar was gone only a few minutes. Tella had regained consciousness, and the nurse had it strapped to a stretcher across the back of Madhar's vehicle. She helped Jim and Madhar carry the stretcher up the ramp.

"How are you doing?" he asked his friend.

"I've been better," Tella replied, obviously in great pain.

Madhar talked quietly with the nurse and then waited for her to leave. Her face was impassive as she gave Jim the bad news.

"Sopha Luca and my bodyguard are missing. Armed factions are facing off on the main road outside the Institute. You have to go quickly."

"Are you sure you don't want to come with us?"

"I have to stay with the students. I can't leave them."

"Good luck. If there's anything I can do, send me a message."

Madhar nodded and strode down the ramp.

Jim launched the flier, set the orbit parameters, and went back to check on Tella.

"Tella? Are you okay?"

The pale eyelids flickered. "No. I have damaged my hips. I may have internal damage."

"What can I do?"

"Use the emergency beacon. It is located under the weapons control panel. Just press the green button. It will open another panel. Follow the directions there."

"Okay. Who does it call?"

"The nearest External Intelligence Agency ship. I don't know what it will be or how far away. I...may not be conscious when it arrives."

"Okay, partner. There's nothing else I can do for you?"

Tella was already unresponsive.

For Jim, there was a long, lonely wait as his craft held position above the Latsin Institute.

For Madhar Nect, it was a long night, huddled in a basement at the Institute with several of her colleagues and three hundred frightened students.

Throughout the night, sporadic weapons fire could be heard around the grounds, around the athletics track, and around the still-smoldering remains of Sopha Luca's flier.

Jim slept sitting in the pilot's seat. He woke up to the sound of silence. It was a kind of silence that in half-sleep was pleasant. Only as he came fully awake, he realized he should be hearing radio traffic. He had set the communications array to sweep the Turcanian radio bands to keep an idea of what was happening down below.

He sat up and turned on the Turcanian TV monitor. There was no transmission. He opened a message session, only to receive an error message that told him to try again later.

He felt blind and deaf.

In the galley, as he drank a juice, he thought of one more device to try. He picked up the Regdenir emergency communicator.

"Hello? This is James Able. Margrev Aplar, are you there?"

There was no reply, but the device seemed to be working.

He tried again. "Margrev Aplar, are you there?"

"Yes, James Able. I am here. Are you well?"

"I am fine. What's happening down there? Why is there no TV transmission or radio traffic?"

"Ah...My colleagues have been busy."

"What do you mean?"

"We learned that the audnir were fighting each other. We do not permit that. They should know better. We have withdrawn all power services until hostilities have ceased."

"Can you do that? Do you have control over all the power supplies?"

"Oh no, only a portion is directly under our control."

"So they should still be partially operating."

"We have been more assertive than we are wont to be."

Jim felt a brief illusion of weightlessness. "Please explain."

"We have placed operatives in all the audnir power stations. We have taken complete control. You may be interested to know we also have Sopha Luca under our protection."

"How did you manage that?"

"Do not underestimate the force of a First Order decision, James Able. When Angara Myourn speaks, many listen. When it comes to keeping the audnir from damaging themselves, there is usually consensus."

Jim shook his head and wondered if he was still asleep. "I don't know what to say. What happens next?"

"The audnir government will be required to meet with the First Order. You will be required to address the assembly."

Jim looked at the communicator, but it was real and solid. "Required to...? When?"

"We will contact you."

"But..."

The Regdenir had ended the call.

While he waited for word from the moon below, Jim began a long-range scan, watching for any EIA craft to respond to his alarm call. There were no ships anywhere nearby.

The atmosphere of TMV was clearing. The ozone columns had

dissipated. There were still large fires burning at some of Sopha's target sites. Jim wondered whether to go down and try to put them out. It was unrealistic. That wasn't a job for a small flier. He grieved for the Maggnir. There was no way of telling how many the Regdenir had killed. He continued to feel the nagging urge to do something to help.

He thought about the equipment Sopha had used. If the base unit had been on board the flier, all the information collected about the Maggnir had been destroyed. It was possible that the data was somewhere hidden with one of his supporters. Both sides should have access to it, if the data did survive. Jim resolved to find out; this, at least, was something he could do.

Knowing the frequency in use between the scanning nodes, Jim could easily put together what looked to the scanners like a diagnostic test message. He transmitted the message and watched his map of TMV-I light up with twenty-five points of light. He stored each reply and read through the data streams. He knew twenty-four of them should be from remote scanning nodes that had, in their various combinations, provided the accuracy that Sopha had needed. One of the nodes, Tella had been sure, was on board the flier and, so, would have been in no condition to reply. Jim knew one reply had to come from the base unit. It was in the storage of this unit that the recorded data from each scan should still be available.

"Got you!" he said to the sixteenth reply.

He consulted his maps of the Turcanian cities.

"Arva? What's in Arva?"

He picked up the Turcanian communicator again.

"Margrev Aplar? Are you there?"

"Greetings, James Able."

"I have identified the locations of all the equipment that Sopha Luca was using. There is one in particular that I need you to secure. It must not be touched or switched off."

"Very well. We have already gained much of this information. Which one are you concerned about?"

"It's in Arva."

"Yes, in Sopha Luca's own home."

"Really? I thought he lived in Oppudim."

"Perhaps it is truer to say he worked there, rather than lived there. His family home is in Arva."

"Oh, I see."

"Is there anything you require us to do with the device in Arva?"

Jim replied, "I'd like to extract the information it contains. As long as it remains undisturbed, I can do it any time."

"Very well, perhaps after our meeting."

"Okay. Any word on the meeting yet?"

"Soon, James Able. You must have patience in this matter."

"Fine," Jim said but did not mean.

Two hours later, Jim received a call on the flier's main communications system.

"This is EIA Flight A92. Please state the nature of your emergency."

"Hello? This is James Able of the OEA. We have an injured...party on board, can you assist?"

"Please identify the injured party."

"R546."

While he waited for a reply, Jim tried to work out what he could from the voice. It was deep and powerful. It wasn't human. He guessed this was another of the code-only operatives.

"Stand by for docking."

"Wait a minute. What do you mean 'docking'?"

"Stand by for docking. Do not engage any engines or thrusters during the docking procedure."

"Okay. If you're sure."

While he waited, Jim looked out a window. The approaching craft was huge. It was a misshapen black lump. It looked like a combination of several unrelated craft that had come together in some interplanetary pileup. He watched a docking tube weave its way from the monster's nearest extremity to the back of the flier.

He went to greet his visitor.

The docking hatch opened to allow a machine to roll forward into the flier. Jim thought it looked like an automated toilet cleaner.

"What are you?" he said to it.

"Diagnostic unit D47. Please identify the patient."

Jim waved the machine through to Tella. It drew up alongside Tella, and immediately several probes extended over the Neraffan's still frame.

"Transmitting," said the unit.

Jim heard the voice over the communications unit again. "James Able."

"Able here."

"R546 has sustained skeletal trauma requiring surgery."

"Do you have the onboard facilities for that?" Jim asked.

"R546 is to be transferred to this vessel."

Jim gritted his teeth. He was reluctant to see his friend taken away like this, but he knew there was no alternative. He couldn't do anything for it.

"Do I get a receipt?"

There was a long pause.

"No."

Obviously, this race was not as in tune with human humor as Tella.

A floating platform pushed its way through the docking hatch and hovered next to the diagnostic unit. Jim hauled the Neraffan onto it. The diagnostic unit extended an arm, connected to the platform, and led it back through the docking hatch.

"I didn't mean it, Tella! I'll let you get me drunk again."

The hatch closed.

CHAPTER FIFTEEN

Jim lay back in the pilot's seat. His mind was drifting. He didn't know the flight procedures to land back at the EIA secure terminal. He'd worry about that when he got there. He didn't know how to reach Tella when he got back to Earth. He doubted the EIA would even admit Tella's existence, let alone give out its address. It troubled him. Tella was an unexpected friend. Jim didn't have enough friends to lightly lose one. He felt angry and sad about both Tella and the Maggnir.

If only I'd been quicker! If only I'd stopped Sopha before he'd started!

He slept again for several hours. The radio transmissions returned sometime during his sleep. He awoke half-hearing news about troops on street corners and curfews. By the time he had showered and eaten breakfast, he could hear that order had been restored.

"Perhaps someone has shown some backbone? Apart," he said wryly to himself, "from Angara Myourn."

He tried to send a message to Madhar, but the system was still unavailable. He considered calling the Regdenir but didn't want to be told he should be patient again.

An idea occurred to him.

If I reconfigure the scanners to the correct frequency, imitate the destroyed node from Sopha's array, and go over to TMV-Two, I can use his entire array to look at the current state of the Maggnir. And then run a comparison with Sopha's accumulated data. Surely the Turcanians will want to know what had happened on Beauty?

He nudged the flier out of orbit and made the short trip to the second moon. He spent an hour mapping the heat sources on the planet.

The Regdenir communicator came to life.

"James Able?"

"This is he."

"Greetings, James Able, this is Margrev Aplar. The scanning devices are behaving in a different manner."

"Ah, yes. I am using them."

"Please explain."

"I'm taking readings of Main-umm-Beauty. I guessed you would need to know what damage Sopha Luca had done."

The Regdenir was silent long enough for Jim's heart to sink.

"Please cease all such activities. We must consult with the First Order before any such thing is done again."

"Margrev, I'm only recording data. What possible objection could they have?"

There was another silence on the other end.

"James Able, please remember you are our guest. We are not yet ready to allow any...anyone to use such equipment or to observe Beauty in such a manner. We must consult with the First Order."

Jim sighed and terminated the scanning.

"Very well. I'm powering down."

"Thank you."

"Any news for me?"

"The audnir are calm once more. We are controlling the restoration of power. The meeting will take place soon. Be patient, James Able, be patient."

As he ended the call, Jim brought his fist down on the console and shouted, "Stupid bastards!"

He decided to return to TMV-I via TMV. He did as comprehensive a planetary sweep as he could using the flier's sensors. It would not have the accuracy of the wide array that Sopha had assembled, but there might be something to see. Jim thought if no one else wanted to know what damage had been done, he did.

When he was once more in orbit around TMV-I, he connected to Sopha's base controller and uploaded its entire database. He set up the parameters for a search-and-compare analysis. The computer gave a runtime estimate of twenty hours. He started it and sat back with an angry sigh.

"James Able?"

"This is he."

"Greetings, James Able. This is Margrev Aplar. The message system is restored. You will find a message for you."

"Okay, what does it say?"

"It was not I who sent it."

"I'll check it."

"We will meet again soon."

g101VnectVlatsinVux

Greetings, James Able of Earth.

It is with great pleasure and excitement that I greet you in the name of our people.

I look forward to meeting with you in person.

I have decided, in the light of recent events, that our people should unite to show one face to our neighbors from other worlds.

I request that you join us for an introductory meeting at the Great Hall of the Government tomorrow morning.

You will find this in the city of Arnarchara.

I will arrange for City Lawn to the west of the Great Hall to be cleared for your landing.

Two cultural ambassadors will be assigned to you upon your

arrival to guide you and answer any questions you may have before the meeting.

jisporaVflacVmeblishVnrc

———

jisporaVflacVmeblishVnrc
Greetings, Jispora Flac.

It is with great pleasure that I accept your most gracious invitation.

I, too, look forward to our first meeting.

James Able
g101VnectVlatsinVux

———

madharVnectVlatsinVux
Greetings, Madhar Nect.

I am relieved to see order has returned.

Are you okay?

I have received my summons to the Great Hall of Government. Will you be there?

g101VnectVlatsinVux

———

margrevVaplarVregde2Vopp
Greetings, Margrev Aplar.

I am glad to see your efforts have been successful.

What can you tell me about the meeting to which I have been invited?

g101VnectVlatsinVux

———

g101VnectVlatsinVux

Greetings, James Able.

Yes, our efforts have been rewarded with success.

I will be answering your questions when you land in Arnarchara tomorrow.

margrevVaplarVregde2Vopp

⬚▭

"Okay, cultural ambassador," Jim said to the screen. "So, the Regdenir are taking a high profile, are they?"

⬚▭

g101VnectVlatsinVux

Greetings, Jim Able.

Perhaps I should be grateful that I am alive, and even grateful to the tree-climbers that they still hold some influence.

But then, I just lost out on a huge TV deal to my rivals in the news organization. It is they who will cover the first official visit of an alien to our people, not *Science World*.

Life is cruel sometimes, Jim Able.

How is your partner? Are its injuries severe? Will it be with us tomorrow?

madharVnectVlatsinVux

⬚▭

madharVnectVlatsinVux

Greetings, Madhar Nect.

Tella was badly injured and transferred to another craft with better facilities than this one. I have hopes that Tella will survive.

How are relations with the Regdenir? I hear they will have a role in tomorrow's meeting.

g101VnectVlatsinVux

g101VnectVlatsinVux

Greetings, Jim Able.

I would rather talk to you in person about the Regdenir.

Their role in all this is still not entirely clear. I, too, hear they will be represented, but news is hard to come by. They seemed to have backed the Meblish party. I doubt this will be sustainable. But "politics is the art of uncertainty," as one of our former chairs used to say.

We will meet again tomorrow, spaceman.

madharVnectVlatsinVux

Jim felt uncomfortable about being the center of an official, televised, worldwide event. That wasn't his job. He had only come to see about a minor trade matter.

I should be asking Liz to send a full diplomatic first contact mission.

"It's too late to back out now," he muttered under his breath. He went to shave and dress in something like a uniform.

Around midmorning, he landed on City Lawn. The crowd was enormous. The TV crews were covering every angle. As he walked down the ramp, he could hear the buzzing of the crowd mixing with occasional cheering. He felt to check that the remote unit for the flier was still tied to his belt.

Madhar Nect and Margrev Aplar were waiting for him. The Regdenir was dressed, as always, in his hooded blue cloak. The scientist was in an odd, hooded cloak of her own. It was a rust-brown color with a red diagonal stripe. She looked uncomfortable in it.

"Greetings, James Able of Earth," began Margrev Aplar. "I believe you already know the Nooc of Gullara, Madhar Nect?"

"Indeed, yes," Jim said with a small bow. He added quietly to Madhar, "The what?"

Madhar shifted her feet and looked down. "It's an honorary title. It means I once advised an alliance chair about science. Don't let it worry you." She waved her hand to dismiss the matter.

Margrev continued, "Please come with us, and we will take you into the Great Hall."

Madhar added under her breath, "Wave to the cameras, Jim. Your public is watching you."

"Don't make it worse than it already is!"

Jim waved to the crowd and then to the nearest camera.

The Great Hall of the Government seemed out of place in what Jim knew of Turcanian society. It was ornate, old, and slightly musty-smelling. Madhar told him it was the crowning achievement of the unification movement, which had brought an end to the local wars that scarred most of their history.

The Regdenir only made one comment. "'Unification' was, and is, an exaggeration."

Madhar responded, "At least now, most of the time, we only fight with votes."

"And in doing so, you let the corporations become independent tribes. In replacing the old political entities, they begin again to make endless war."

The three stopped along a long wood-paneled corridor.

"Look," replied Madhar testily. "I'm not a politician, nor I hear, are you."

"Nor am I," said Jim.

Margrev Aplar looked as though he might punch the scientist in the face.

"Your point?"

"It's not our place to sort out this kind of mess. But you know very well there's a lot of history here that can't be just swept away."

"That is correct," he replied, "if you refer to Regdenir history!"

"Cool it, you two," interrupted Jim. "You've got the rest of your lives to make peace. I just want to say 'Hello' and be on my way."

The thought of Jim's leaving affected them both. Aplar closed his eyes and nodded. Madhar smiled sadly. They continued their long walk to the Great Hall.

Doors on either side of the corridor were open. Interested faces watched them pass. A line of soldiers stood at unmoving attention, all the way down to the gold-plated doors.

Two ceremonial guards swung open the doors. Jim saw the expanse of the room open up before him.

The Great Hall of the Government was a huge tiered auditorium. A staircase descended at Jim's feet through row upon row of seated Turcanians. Long curved tables held a monitor for each person. Jim could see his own image showing on hundreds of screens stretching out to his left and right. At the end of the stairs was a stage with two rows of more seated Turcanians in ceremonial robes.

To the right of a podium stood four officials. Madhar whispered their names to Jim as they walked slowly down the steps.

"Jispora Flac to the left, current alliance chair. He's the nearest we have to someone in charge. Next to him is Larspa Culle. She is the leader of the radical movement. They hold this alliance together. Next is Madlen Torespora. He is the oldest statesman we have. Every alliance for the last seventy years has included him—for credibility alone. He's a doddering old fool who just won't die."

Jim's eyes were already locked with the eyes of the fourth figure on the stage.

Margrev took up the commentary. "The final member of the welcoming committee is Almeth Luca of the First Order."

"Did you say Luca?"

"Yes, he is father to Sopha Luca. He is one of the leaders of the First Order."

"Why didn't you tell me?"

"It should not be of concern to you." There was an edge to Margrev's voice that unsettled Jim as much as the stare he was getting from the stage.

"Sorry, Jim," whispered Madhar. "They made me swear not to tell you until it was too late. They were scared you'd back out."

"Damn right."

They reached the stage. Madhar hung back, and Margrev led

Jim across to meet the four dignitaries. Almeth Luca held Jim's hand in a strong grip for a long while. The Regdenir's eyes searched Jim's. No words were spoken, but Jim had a profound sense of having met this Turcanian before. There was a force of personality so strong he could have been telepathic. Jim had expected hostility, but instead, he sensed someone who expected to meet the universe head-on— whatever it had in store—without judgment. Jim was certain he was meeting one of TMV-I's movers and shakers. As he shook hands with the other three, none of them seemed any more than they appeared. Jim wondered what it was in the Regdenir bloodline that could give rise to a figure so impressive.

Margrev motioned Jim to the podium.

He stepped up, and the buzz of the assembly died down. He could see the microphones arranged in a neat row before him. At the corner of his vision, he was aware of the TV cameras. From this position, he could see everything Madhar had told him about Turcanian politics.

The members of the government were assembled by political party. Each party wore robes or sashes of differing colors. It was a bewildering patchwork. There were no blue cloaks in the tiers of seats. Jim guessed that part of the deal that had restored peace was the presence of the Regdenir around the edge of the Great Hall. They were there in large numbers, encircling the chamber. They looked, to Jim, like an army of blue sheepdogs.

The expectant silence surrounded him.

"Here goes!" he said to himself.

"I am James Able, representing the people of the planet Earth. Thank you for this opportunity to address you and to meet with you." He smiled at his audience. "It is important that you know I am not a diplomat. I work merely as an investigator for a department of my government. A small matter brought me here, and that matter has now been resolved, giving us this meeting as a wonderful by-product."

He paused, wondering if that had come out right. "I stand here to confirm what your scientists have been telling you for many years. Life does exist on other worlds. It is possible to travel in space. When you decide to do so, you will find many races out there who will be good friends to you. You will enrich them and they will enrich you. As in any community, there are those who need the discipline of laws. There are institutions in the galactic community to provide that structure. When you decide you wish to know more about this, Earth will gladly send diplomats and advisors to ease your transition."

Jim smiled again and, then, paused to look serious. "The events of the last week need careful thought on your part. To the other races of the galaxy, you are all one. It is hard enough sometimes to keep track of what race lives where; it is impossible to keep track of subdivisions within any one planet's inhabitants. You must, as Jispora Flac has said, 'show one face to your neighbors.' As I look out here on this great assembly, I see that you enjoy and celebrate your differences." A quiet buzz filled the hall. "But in your dealings with other races, everything must be done by consensus and in unity. Different races will come to you. Some will come to trade technology. Some will come to trade biological specimens for agriculture. Some will come to hear your philosophy and to learn at your feet. It will not happen if you are at war with one another. It will not happen if you divide into competing factions."

Jim paused, wondering whether to add any more. As much as this kind of thing was not his job, he was aware of how much he was enjoying it. He felt a surge of confidence, sufficient to speak the thought that came to him with a memory of something Madhar had told him.

"It is time for the a'nir to come out from the shadows."

A roar went up from the Regdenir around the room. Some audnir were nodding and clapping; some were shaking their heads. Not quite understanding the reaction, Jim turned toward Margrev and Madhar. Margrev's eyes were moist, his face turning to Jim in wonder. Madhar approached Jim, laughing and nodding.

The two rows of dignitaries behind him were up and milling around the stage, talking loudly.

Margrev and Madhar took up positions on either side of Jim

and escorted him across the stage to Jispora Flac. The alliance chair looked coldly into Jim's eyes.

"You have been briefed far better than I had anticipated."

"I don't understand," said Jim.

Flac obviously did not believe him. He turned away from Jim and began a conversation with another of his party.

"What's eating him?" Jim asked Madhar.

"Oh, Jim. You've really done it this time," she said, shaking her head.

"What? What did I say?"

"Ask the Regdenir."

Jim was beginning to worry. The Great Hall was still full of the buzz of hundreds of loud voices.

"Margrev?"

"You chose well in quoting scripture, James Able."

"I did? I mean...What scripture?"

"Come. There is a reception awaiting you. You will have another chance to eat our more exotic foods. We can talk there. What a day, James Able, a great day!"

The banquet buffet was laid out in an adjoining hall. The group on stage led the way, but soon many from the assembly filed into the room. They brought the noise of heated discussion with them.

Madhar, Margrev, Larspa Culle (the radical), and Madlen Torespora (the dodderer) stood nibbling various foods with Jim. He got the impression that Torespora was posing for the cameras that had followed him around the room. Jim did not talk much with Culle but could see she had as keen a sense of humor as Madhar.

He tried a couple of times to talk to Margrev, but they were constantly interrupted. Eventually, he became so frustrated that he grabbed the Regdenir by the arm and moved away from the others.

"I really want to know what I said."

"Of course. But wait just a moment."

Jim looked around to where Margrev had pointed. Almeth Luca was sailing through the crowd toward them.

"James Able," Luca said in greeting, bowing slightly.

"Almeth Luca. How is your son?" asked Jim, teeth gritted with tension.

"My son is recovering from his injuries."

"He was hurt?"

"He will recover."

Jim nodded.

Margrev Aplar said, "James Able has asked to understand better why his remarks were of such significance."

Almeth Luca looked into Jim's eyes again with an imperious glance. "It has never been heard that a stranger could quote our scripture." His eyes moved off Jim and into the distance. "The symbol of the eclipse is often used to convey a variety of conditions: a spiritual darkness, an exile, the darkness of ignorance..."

In Sopha's father, Jim could hear the same practiced speech of a teacher that he had heard in the son.

"In *The Prophecies*, there are many such images. Only one uses the word 'a'nir.' It is the Prophecy of Regnarmar. It is accepted that it predicts the dawn of a new age for understanding and peace. It is much disputed whether this is a spiritual or worldly change."

"I understand when you say 'much disputed.' I have seen how you guys discuss things in the Regdekol."

The Regdenir looked at Jim with a fierce expression, a fire lighting in his eyes. It passed in a moment as a broad smile spread across his face. "Hah! I will add allowing you to see the Regdekol to the list of Sopha's sins! When did he show you this prophecy?"

"He didn't. I have never seen it."

"Then how," asked Margrev, "did you know to use the word 'a'nir'?"

"I learned it from Madhar."

This surprised both Regdenir.

"I was talking to her about you all being Turcanians."

"What?"

"What is a Turcanian?"

"Exactly. We call your sun Turcanis Major. Your nearest neighboring star is Turcanis Minor. So we refer to any inhabitant of these systems as Turcanian. Madhar told me you had no modern word that included everyone. Then she remembered 'a'nir.'"

Almeth looked to Margrev, who nodded and said, "Nect's great-grandmother was Fratuin Regdenir. She would have heard it."

Almeth nodded. "It is well said. Your words are timely. For us to take such overt action, as we have, in the affairs of the audnir is rare. Perhaps this is the prophecy being fulfilled. Perhaps this will be the last time we need to act so."

Jim remembered the reaction of Alliance Chair Flac. "Let me ask you: why did Jispora Flac not like my use of the word?"

"He is a weak and pliable politician. Your use of scripture speaks to a stability and a history in which he plays little part and over which he has no control," answered Almeth.

Margrev added, "He will see it not as something that will change our world and the hearts of our people, but simply as a maneuver to endorse our 'faction' over his."

Almeth sighed. "I do not see how we *can* come from under this shadow. Your words have enlivened us, but I fear our imaginations are ahead of our feet."

"It won't be easy. It never is," said Jim.

"Angara Myourn has said it will take much work by the Second Order to turn all hearts and minds from division," said Margrev.

"Indeed," said Almeth, drawing up to his full height. "Then it is clear. James Able, you must arrange that no diplomatic missions be sent until we have completed this work. There must be no more contact while we are not yet a'nir."

Jim's jaw dropped.

"You can't be serious! You can't do that!"

The sound of his raised tone carried into the room, and many faces turned to listen. Madhar was quickly at his side.

"What's wrong, Jim?"

Jim gestured toward Almeth Luca.

"Tell her."

The Regdenir turned to Madhar and said, "We see that the divisions between us, and the divisions within your own people, are such that we cannot yet present 'one face' to our neighbors. Therefore, we will not do so, until we are ready."

Madhar took a moment to comprehend the magnitude of what was being said. "It is not your decision alone!"

"Madhar Nect, let us agree on this first and hold out the hope that we can agree on other things. If we cannot agree on this, the shadow remains over us, and we stumble on our separate ways."

Madhar shook her head abruptly in what Jim guessed was a gesture of irritation. "No, we must open ourselves up to outside influence. That is the only way to achieve what we're all looking for. It does no good to stay bottled up in our own...insularities."

Jim was hot and sensed that something he had drunk had been alcoholic. It inspired him to be direct with his hosts.

"Listen, all of you!" he began, perhaps louder than he had intended. "It's too late for this discussion!"

He tried to think of a clear image. Remembering the trick the TV crew had played on him, he said, "The animal is out of the present already." He noticed the slightly confused expressions but carried on. "I've already been seen by everybody. The idea that you are not alone is already confirmed. There is no going back. Your people will want to look outward. You will all want to travel and trade and learn and teach. And they will want to do that *now*! Accept it. It's going to happen. All you can do is begin to manage the process as speedily as possible. You don't want any more rogue individuals out there without supervision or regulation. No offense meant..."

Jim had not realized how many in the crowded room were listening to him. Apart from some laughter near the door, it seemed the entire gathering was straining to catch his words.

Madhar looked from Jim to Almeth. "He's right."

Almeth frowned and nodded. "My son was incorrect in his assessment of you, James Able. And I understand the danger you thought he represented."

The voice of Larspa Culle interrupted. "We need a government capable of managing such a process and guiding all the people."

Jispora Flac's oratorical tones came from behind her. "And if you think the Regdenir can force a consensus on this assembly, you are sadly mistaken."

The atmosphere chilled.

Almeth spoke directly to Jim. "We know." He gave a subtle nod toward a wide-eyed Madhar. "We know what is required. Leave us with some means of contact. Do not return until we contact you."

Jim understood, in the almost-unnoticed nod to his friend, that Almeth was acknowledging that a new alliance had formed between the religious and the scientific forces of TMV-I. Jim nodded, almost feeling sorry for Jispora Flac and his kind.

The reception was over soon after. Jispora Flac said nothing further to him. But before Jim could leave, he had to be introduced to a seemingly endless line of politicians, all needing to have their pictures taken with him.

Jim invited Madhar, Margrev, and Almeth into his flier before he took off.

"I've a few things to give you before I go."

He opened a box full of Standard Language Tutors.

"Please take as many of these as you like. There is a section on how to copy them."

"I've already got it on the syllabus," said Madhar.

"We will take them," said Margrev.

"I have something else." Jim pulled out two data storage devices. "Do you think you can get the data off these? They are like the ones in the scanners."

Madhar shook her head. "I doubt it."

Almeth looked at them and said, "Perhaps. I can ask our technicians to examine them."

"When you do, share it with Madhar."

"Of course," the Regdenir nodded.

Margrev asked, "What do they contain?"

Jim glanced at Almeth. "They are before and after images of Beauty. On here, you can see all the information Sopha gathered on the Maggnir from his scanners. And everything I was able to gather afterward."

The Regdenir had impassive expressions, either unwilling or

unable to express their feelings. Almeth reached out to take the units. In a faint voice he said, "We must incorporate all of this into the Regdekol. James Able, it is well done."

Jim smiled and said, "You're welcome."

Madhar laughed and said, "What a journey that was, Jim!"

Jim frowned and asked, "What do you mean?"

The scientist nodded toward Almeth Luca. "You're one of the first people in an age to come so close to receiving a compliment from a Regdenir!"

EPILOGUE AND PROLOGUE

Three months later, Jim was sitting in a bar. Liz Curacao had fired him as soon as she read his report.

Something, perhaps several things, had made it clear to her that he would not change. She could no longer manage him; he had to go.

He went. And he went into a deep depression. Dawkins transferred him to another counselor.

This bar was his current favorite. He had a fresh beer waiting expectantly in front of him. A hand reached out from his right and took the glass. The pale flesh glowed amber, and small dots rose up the side of the hand.

"Tella!"

"Jim, you're a mess!"

"It's good to see you too! You've recovered?"

"Better than you, it seems."

"Yeah, well...I've been a bit down lately."

"Then pick yourself up—quickly!"

"What's happening?"

"You're late."

"Late for what?"

"For your interview."

"What interview?"

"With me."

"What are you talking about?"

"I have a job opening. You are the preferred candidate."

"You're joking!"

Tella's impassive face spread into a pale grin. "I never joke about work. The job is yours. Just sober up, clean up, and turn up."

"I...I don't know what to say."

"Since when has Jim Able not had the right words for the occasion?"

Jim smiled and shook his head. A fragment of Quavvour had just reappeared in his life.

FIRST CONTACT CLAIM FORM

Office of External Affairs
Department of Extra-Solar Activities

CONFIDENTIAL

FC01 - Processing

Assigned to: E. Curacao

Introduction Form – FC01

Reported: January 12, 2200

Claimant Name (original): JAMES ABLE

Claimant Name (phonetic, if required):

Describe yourself:

I am a former employee of the Office of External Affairs.
I was dismissed for cause: specifically, "acting in a private capacity whilst on duty."
If this is true then the Office will have no difficulty accepting this application from me as an independent individual, who made contact with a new race to Earth's ultimate benefit.

Describe the nature of the First Contact:

During 2199 I had two trips to the primary moon of Turcanis Major V, in pursuit of a lone trader Sopha Luca. There were two competing claims from individuals who had dealings with him. However, he had no intention of establishing any relations with anyone. Neither claim has been paid.

Through my own efforts, and in the view of my former boss in an independent capacity, I secured a working relationship with both the scientific, religious, and political authorities on TMV-I.

I am informed by legal counsel that under the terms governing FC claims, I am the one and only person who can rightly be said to have made this introduction.

Declaration:

I believe myself to be the first person to introduce this new race to the Earth and claim all fees and rewards previously published in pursuance of this introduction.

I give my signature to this document in affirmation of all its contents:

*Oh FFS!
Can you believe this?
Liz*

Sign here: *James Able*

Note: This form may only be used for First Contact Claims for the introduction fees current at time of signature. For detail of current fees contact issuing authority. For any other claims Do NOT USE THIS FORM as this will delay processing.

For Office use only

Authorized for payment

Date:

By the authority of the Secretary of the Office of Expansion Services

Assistant to the Secretary

Jim Able Offworld is for readers who enjoy quirky aliens, flawed humans, and heroes who work in outer space. Explore the galaxy with Jim as he navigates the hidden schemes of criminals, governments, interplanetary corporations, and his own frenemies.

Book One: Beauty Rising

To Do: Find alien, avoid starting war, submit expenses

Jim's accidental and dangerous first contact on Turcanis Major V-I.

Book Two: Larc Ascending

To Do: Tail drone, destroy space fleet, submit expenses

An unfolding mystery, a conflict between the neighboring planets of the Tanna system, and the secret that ties them together.

Book Three: Time

To Do: Rescue renowned artist, return time machine, change careers.

The past interrupts the present in the form of a troubling inheritance from Jim's father leaving Jim to deal with the consequences of an action he has yet to take.

Available at edcharlton.com

THE ALERONDE TRILOGY

The Aleronde Trilogy - Three very different books.

One epic sci-fi tale.

Visitors from Earth witness the shocking downfall of Aleronde. They share an unexpected role in this catastrophe with a mysterious figure from the past who unpicks the fabric of the Aleronden empire with that most dangerous thing: an idea.

Read *Aleronde the Great* and its two prequels, *The Problem with Uncle Teddy's Memoir* and *Saint John's Ambulatory*.

The Problem with Uncle Teddy's Memoir tells—through letters, emails, and Uncle Teddy's own manuscript—a troubling tale of empire, slavery, and betrayal. Reading the memoir forces two friends to reexamine their childhood experiences of abduction.

Saint John's Ambulatory reads like a murder mystery, but there are aliens in every shadow. Only one man has evidence of extraterrestrials on Earth, but now, he's dead.

In *Aleronde the Great*, the significance of Uncle Teddy's memoir and the Ambulatory are revealed, and one small act of kindness unleashes trouble of galactic proportions.

The Aleronde Trilogy at edcharlton.com

How to murder someone on a space station

and get away with it

Hoyle Station is a murder mystery with a cast of thousands, some of them human.

And there are many questions. How has a member of Earth's Historical Guild so completely vanished? Are the Recorders who run the business of the station as helpful as they seem? Who are the aliens watching from the dark of space?

Hoyle Station

Subscribe to Ed's free monthly newsletter!